ABOUT THE AUTHOR

Born in Shanghai to a writer and an actress, Geling Yan herself began writing in the late 1970s as a war correspondent covering the Sino-Vietnamese border conflicts. Her first novel was published in China in 1985. In 1989, following the massacre at Tiananmen Square, she left China for the United States. Since then, two of her works have been made into films and a collection of her short fiction was translated into English. She has won many awards, both in China and the U.S. She now lives in San Francisco.

ABOUT THE TRANSLATOR

Cathy Silber teaches Chinese language and literature at Williams College. She has been translating Chinese prose and poetry into English for nearly twenty years. A recipient of awards from the Bunting Fellowship Program at the Radcliffe Institute for Advanced Study and the American Council of Learned Societies, she is at work on a book about literature written in *nushu*, the Chinese women's script.

THE
LOST
DAUGHTER
OF
HAPPINESS

Geling Yan

TRANSLATED BY
CATHY SILBER

faber and faber

First published in the United States in 2001
by Hyperion 77 w.66th Street, New York, New York 10023-6298

First published in the United Kingdom in 2001
by Faber and Faber Limited
3 Queen Square London WCIN 3AU

This paperback edition published in 2002

Printed in England by Mackays of Chatham plc, Chatham, Kent

A CIP record for this book
is available from the British Library

ISBN 0-571-20766-9

2 4 6 8 10 9 7 5 3

To Larry

THE LOST DAUGHTER
OF HAPPINESS

THIS IS WHO YOU ARE.

The one dressed in red, slowly rising from the creaking bamboo bed, is you. The embroidery on your satin padded jacket must weigh ten catties; the parts stitched most densely are as hard as ice, or armor. From a distance of one hundred and twenty years, I am amazed by the needlework, so thoroughly beyond me.

Let me raise your chin a bit here, and bring your lips into the dim light. That's it, just right. Now I can see your whole face clearly. Don't worry—others will just find exotic the face you consider too square. To the novelty seekers of your day, your every flaw was a distinction.

Now turn around, just like all those times on the auction block. You're used to the auction; that's where pretty whores like you come to know their worth. I found pictures of those auctions in some books about Chinatown—dozens of female bodies, totally naked, their beauty in sharp relief against the surrounding gloom.

You're nothing like the other girls on auction. First of all, you lived past twenty. This is a miracle. I looked through all one hundred and sixty of those books and you were the only one to live so long. The other girls in your line of work started losing their hair at eighteen, their teeth at nineteen, and by twenty, with their vacant eyes and decrepit faces, they were as good as dead, silent as dust.

But you're *nothing* like them.

Don't be so eager to show off your feet. I know they're less than four inches long: two mummified magnolia buds. I'll let you show them later. After all, you're not like that woman who lived at 129 Clay Street from 1890 to 1940 and made her living putting her four-inch golden lotuses on display. Several thousand tourists a day would shuffle reverently past her door, looking at the way her dead toes had been broken clean under and now curled into the soles of her feet. Most of them came from the more genteel East Coast, though some even came from the other side of the Atlantic, just to pay homage to a vestige of antiquity on a real live body. In the deformity and decay of those feet, they could read the *Orient*.

I know who you were: a twenty-year-old prostitute, one of a succession of three thousand prostitutes from China. When you stepped upon these golden shores, you were a fully grown woman. You had no skills, no seductive charms, not a trace of lust in your eyes. People could sense your distinctive simplicity the moment they met you. In an instant, you could make any man feel as if it were his wedding night.

So you were a born prostitute, a good-as-new bride.

On a summer day in the late 1860s, there's a rather large girl standing in a barred window on a narrow lane in San Francisco's Chinatown, and that's you.

You have a strange name: Fusang. You're not from the Canton delta, so your price is 30 percent higher than those girls with names like Pearl, Silky, or Snapper, who had a hard time proving themselves unsullied by foreign sailors on shore.

Now look at me, a writer here in the late twentieth century. You want to know whether the same thing brought me to Gold Mountain. I've never known what made me take that stride across the Pacific. We've all got ready answers—that we came for freedom, knowledge, wealth—but really we have no idea what we're after.

Some call us fifth-wave Chinese immigrants.

You're wondering why I singled you out. You don't know that foreign historians wrote about you in these one hundred and sixty histories of the Chinese in San Francisco that no one else has bothered to read. These writers are totally serious when they say things like: "When the famous, or perhaps we should say infamous, Chinese prostitute Fusang appeared in all her finery, gentlemen were so stirred they could not help but doff their hats to her." And: "The consensus on this Chinese prostitute, considered such an anomaly, confirmed that she was essentially the same as her Western counterparts and showed no anatomical abnormalities."

You know I too am auctioning you.

You turn around again, and now I see the huge bun at the back of your head, with a hairpin of white jade and a garland of pink silk flowers starting behind your left ear and looped down around half the bun. Several years from now, the depths of this bun will hide a brass button belonging to Chris, that white boy.

The first time he saw you, when he first thought of buying your services, he was only twelve.

Let's take a look at you from the very beginning. Very good: The hazy distance between us has thinned and all of a sudden you're right here.

Your fourteen-year-old colleagues instructed you to "market" yourself: If you don't get work, Fusang, you won't get supper and you'll be whipped naked. Your juniors in the field considered you worthless—you didn't know how to sell yourself; you didn't know how to make eyes at the men outside the window.

The histories describe this marketing in detail: "Chinese prostitutes employed their own unique ways of attracting customers: 'Nice Chinese girl, hey mister, come on in and see, your daddy he just go out! . . .' 'Two bittee lookee, fol bittee feelee, six bittee do-ee! . . .' 'Chinese girly, fresh off boat, good girly, only thirty cent! . . .' Every now and then, moved by such explicit language and cheap prices, someone would turn back, pause, and pick out one of those children, one much like the next."

You didn't hawk yourself. Whenever a man looked at you, you smiled at him, hesitantly at first, and then so wholeheartedly you made him feel you were wild about him and perfectly content with your life.

It was probably your smile that made these men realize you were no ordinary goods. Someone slows before your window. Bigger and taller than most, you rise from the creaky bamboo bed. The slight delay in your movements makes you seem almost dignified.

People could forget for a moment that you were a caged prostitute for sale.

This is what you were like when you first arrived in San Francisco. I certainly won't let people confuse you with any of the other three thousand whores from China.

EVENING FOG CAME ASHORE from the sea, dampening the dirt on the streets, growing heavier, settling. The dust that caught in Fusang's throat was no longer coming in the window.

A bit cold, a bit tired, a bit hungry, she was watching the buggy lanterns jouncing along.

Next door was fourteen-year-old Doughface, whose voice by now was as hoarse as the sound of ripping cloth. Three little white devils walked by, no more than eleven or twelve. Hearing Doughface call out, they pressed their dirty fingers to their throats to mimic her voice, the sound of their laughter like paper rattling in the wind.

Doughface tried again, Hurry up, come on in, your daddy he just go out!

The little white devils tore open their shirts like brutes, exposing their funny-looking navels. They begged her to unbutton her blouse.

She dickered over the price while fanning her collar open and shut. Her breasts looked like two swollen mosquito bites. She wasn't terribly pretty to begin with and the pockmarks on her face were as deep as raindrops in sand.

Her bamboo bed started singing, creaking out a rhythm. She would eat tonight.

Fusang left the window. The room was so small that with only four steps she had reached the curtain on the other side, where several flies hung, too cold to move. The flowers embroidered on the curtain had not yet faded. She lifted the curtain, with its filth and red flowers and green leaves and flies, stepped inside, raised and secured her skirt, and lowered herself over the copper chamber pot.

The water in the wash basin beside the chamber pot was still clean—no customers. All the prostitutes here told Fusang, You've got to wash yourself as soon as the john leaves, or else you'll stink to high heaven.

On a little bamboo stand were soap, face powder, and rouge. Fusang rubbed a little rouge on her lips. She liked the fruit-sweet taste.

Amah, the madam, pushed open the door and entered, calling to Fusang in a voice as burnt as dregs of cooking fat. Amah Mei carried around a big brass kettle all day, pouring fresh water into the wash basins in every room.

Fusang got up from the chamber pot, a little sorry to leave the circle of warmth she'd made while sitting there.

Amah, parting the curtain with her backside, poured some water into the basin and said, Still no customers? I keep forking out for your rice and salt fish, and what do I get in return? She raised her eyebrows and sighed with a smile at Fusang. What's the matter? You got a lump of gold in your mouth? Afraid it'll fall out if you talk?

Fusang smiled back and said nothing.

At midnight, take off your clothes and wait in my room. The boss wants to give you a good beating. You hear me?

Fusang said she heard.

Don't forget to fasten your hair up tight, Amah continued. Don't let him pull your hair. Once he pulls a girl's hair, he's an addict. He can't stop beating her. He loses track of how much he's beaten her. He'll beat her to death and not even know it.

I won't forget.

Your hair is so thick, Amah said. What a great head of hair—you go through three ounces of my hair oil a day. Hey, what are you crying about?

Nothing, nothing, Fusang said, shaking her head. I'm just hungry.

No you're not. When you're hungry you can't pee and I just heard you take a long one.

Fusang wanted to ask Amah for some better sandalwood incense, but the sound of Doughface seeing off her john distracted her.

Amah said, You've got to do a better job. You're already twenty. Other girls are household names by your age. If you don't get a customer soon, I'm selling you off next month and that's all there is to it.

WHIPPED, AND THEN SALVED, Fusang walked slowly down the dark hall toward the faint yellow light. When she reached the third door, she relaxed a bit. Her lash wounds were starting to cool off. She entered the dining room, which contained a big table with sixteen chairs. The table had been cleared, though here and there a fish bone or scrap of vegetable stuck to its surface. A boiled fleshy fish head, big as a piglet's, lay in an earthenware pot. Deep red blood still clung to its lips.

Fusang wondered if Amah had been serious when she'd said she'd sell her. After all, she was willing to part with such a big fish head for her. Fusang shooed a few cockroaches from beneath the lip of the pot, sat down, took her feet from beneath her skirt, and rested them on the chair across from her.

She broke the fish head open and lifted it piece by piece into her mouth.

Suddenly, Amah shouted from the hall, Fusang, you've got a customer!

She answered her, then pulled out a handkerchief and wiped the sweat from the tip of her nose. She heard Amah shout, Fusang, can't you hear me when I'm calling you? What've you been doing, stuffing food in your ears?

Fusang got up and answered more loudly as she readjusted her skirt and walked toward her room.

She was flustered and glad, almost skipping. She'd been waiting for a customer for a whole month and now that he was here, shouldn't she be flustered and glad?

When she reached her room, she jumped back in shock, figuring she must have barged through the wrong door. Four red candles were burning and wisps of top-grade sandalwood incense smoke were circling into a net, weaving into a curtain, the fragrance so heavy she squinted.

Tongues of candle flame shimmied and the golden-red space of the whole room turned unstable. Fusang thought Amah must like her after all, to part with such good candles and incense.

She faced the mirror, her cheeks aflame. She tidied her forelocks with her comb, then flung it down with a clatter, grabbed the flowers and stuck them into her hair. What would her first man be like? She didn't dare turn around. Mangy? Crippled? One-eyed? Harelipped? As she started to smile, the door pushed open with a creak.

Quietly, he stepped in.

Fusang saw him in the mirror. She bit her lip so hard she swallowed some rouge.

He didn't even smile. He just stood there in the doorway, watching her get up from her stool. He stared at her with disbelief.

Fusang quickly sized him up. He wasn't much shorter than she was, the top of his head coming up to her ears, but the contours of his face were still childlike, so he seemed shorter and smaller.

She didn't know that countless times this boy had hidden in the shadows of walls and trees to watch her. She was the strangest thing he'd ever seen. Her every movement made him bite his thumb to the point of pain.

She didn't know that he used a little round mirror to savor every part of her. He had learned as a child to use this mirror to capture any scene in the world as his own, however momentary, private possession.

As far as Fusang was concerned, he was just a boy, another little white devil not much different from Doughface's johns. Still, she made up her mind to give him good service.

She took off the padded jacket that must have consumed ten catties of silk floss. This was the only such jacket in the whole brothel, given to each girl to wear with her first customer.

Chris, the boy said. My name is Christopher. Call me Chris. He forced his voice to sound rough and low to make himself seem an old hand at this.

Fusang said with a curtsy, My name is Fusang.

He had found out her name a long time ago.

Fusang went on to say, Please have a seat, have some tea, will you be staying the night, sir? She knew a total of twenty words in English.

His eyes wide with wonder, Chris took in the furnishings of the room.

The curling incense smoke made their shabbiness seem appropriate.

She brought over a pot of freshly brewed tea and a plate of roasted watermelon seeds dyed the color of blood. These were the usual refreshments. They rarely served alcohol because it led to violence and the woman was left beaten to a pulp and useless.

The table was covered with a tablecloth. The two bamboo chairs, one on each side, had embroidered cushions on their seats, gray cotton stuffing showing through the worn corners. Across from the table was a bamboo bed, above which hung a pink bed curtain, though the wrinkled parts were no longer pink but stained a yellowish gray by incense smoke. The walls were also painted pink and they too were smoke-stained. Chris could not conceal the curiosity in his eyes—that invasive curiosity of twelve-year-old boys.

Fusang poured the tea. The glugging sound made the boy turn to look at her.

She tilted her head as she poured and her earrings ducked and trembled as if afflicted with a painful itch. As she turned to smile at him, the tea missed the cup. The silvery smoke made her seem very far away.

Fusang sat down, adjusted her skirt, and propped one tiny pointed red foot on top of the other.

Chris had no trouble keeping his eyes on those feet. All the legends about them were now proven, right before his very eyes. Such deformed yet beautiful things really did exist!

Still in shock, he sat down and lifted his cup. He just kept looking at her.

Twisting open the button loop at her collar, Fusang asked him again if he was staying the night.

He said he wasn't. He was looking at the opening in her worn silk blouse. Such delicate skin. Her hand continued on down, undoing buttons. Suddenly she stopped, seeing him pulling back his tongue, scalded by the tea. She reached over to take the cup and began to blow on the tea.

Chris had never seen such a thing. Her pursed lips and lowered lashes lent her face all the gentleness of a mother. Her translucent silk blouse shimmered with every breath she blew. The candlelight accentuated the shapes and movements of the body underneath. She bent her neck, tilted the cup, and touched her lips briefly to the surface of the tea. And then she wiped her lips with the back of one hand and returned the cup to him with the other. She barely smiled.

He was sure he'd never seen a woman do such things

before. He just stared. He couldn't figure out what made her movements so tempting—such a new and different temptation.

Fusang waited a moment, with a fairly good idea of what he was going through. She crossed the room and trimmed a candle wick that didn't need it. Then, instead of returning to her seat, she walked over and stood before him. Her smile wasn't the sort she'd ordinarily give a twelve-year-old boy. As if a boy his age deserved such a smile, such wholehearted anticipation.

Chris didn't move. She was standing two feet in front of him, making it so easy for him, yet he didn't move. He felt her hand coming toward him and stop on his shoulder. He felt her full round breasts rise in expectation. And he couldn't move.

At this point, Fusang resorted to saying the dirtiest English words she knew. Her lips and tongue struggled with the earnestness of her effort to make each sound. She said these words with complete sincerity.

They lost their meanings instantly. The heart behind the words was so innocent that each syllable became something entirely unfamiliar. The effect was enchanting.

She massaged his earlobes with her fingers, earlobes as tender as tiny buds, so soft her heart trembled.

She really wasn't much taller than he was; she just seemed to be because her body was so developed. When she embraced him, his lips reached her face easily.

Smiling, she pulled away, walked over to the dressing

table, and removed her earrings, bracelets, necklace, and hairpins. To Chris, these trinkets brought to mind all the mysteries of the Orient and the ornate intricacies of antiques. Finally, her black hair fell like water, as black and impenetrable as the sky before time began.

She sat down on the bamboo bed, which creaked with her weight, and smoothed the sheet beside her.

The role of the bed suddenly dawned on Chris. The whole filthy building was filled with the banging and creaking of those beds. He got a good look at Fusang's feet. She had taken off her red shoes and then the semi-sheer pink stockings with two tiny holes in them.

She slowly moved her feet to the edge of the bed.

Chris couldn't believe they were real. He moved closer to them. They seemed to belong to a stage of evolution no one had ever imagined. Unaware of what he was doing, he knelt beside the bed and reached out and touched them. They looked like fishtails—the most sensitive, vulnerable part. How could they be feet? He kept his touch extremely light, afraid they would melt and die.

Fusang had arranged her hair, and was watching him, her whole body ready.

He suddenly smiled. The smile of a boy who thinks he's gotten to the bottom of a big mystery.

Amah yelled from the doorway, Excuse me, sir, are you planning to stay the night?

YOU HAD THOUGHT OF EVERYTHING: mangy, crippled, one-eyed. But you were shocked when you turned to the creaking door. You never imagined such a little kid. You bit your lip, bit the sharp sweetness of rouge. The twelve-year-old john had come in.

You could tell he'd dressed up; he wore a gold chain on his vest, a handkerchief in his breast pocket, and his straw-colored hair was slicked back with so much oil that it looked like a cap. You saw right through him from the start. Twelve, tops. Even being white couldn't help disguise his age. The curiosity in his pale blue eyes was almost cruel. Such curiosity is only found in boys that age.

It's hard to say what he looked like. All boys have the same vaguely shaped mouth. From suckling at the breast to sucking hard candy, certain instincts remain on the lips. This was the mouth that fed his ravenous curiosity: a mouth in transition, a mouth that devoured so many fairy tales and adventure stories. You were his fairy tale. Your cavelike room was a distant kingdom, and your every movement had magical powers. The *Orient*—the word alone was enough to become the origin of all mysteries, at least as far as this twelve-year-old boy was concerned.

Once you got over your shock, you pretended you couldn't tell how young he was. You wouldn't cut a single corner with him, you decided. You smiled at him as if he were a man every bit your match. You never thought of him as just one of the hundreds of little white devils who came to the Chinatown brothels looking for cheap thrills.

Let me tell you about that: In a single year, over two thousand white boys between the ages of eight and fourteen entertained themselves with Chinese prostitutes. One of my books calls it "a most unusual social phenomenon. . .a contagion running rampant through morality and decency.. . .Fifty percent of the boys visited Chinese brothels on a regular basis, and ninety percent used their lunch money or candy allowance. . . ."

I'm looking at you in the candlelight. There's nothing cheap about you, even though all my sources keep insisting the "cheapness" of Chinese prostitutes is what attracted white boys. Just the way the cheap restaurants, housewares, and produce of Chinatown today attract penniless new immigrants like me, as well as tourists from all over the world.

Now you are walking step by step toward him, this twelve-year-old white devil named Chris. Your steady step makes you seem big and tall, ripe to the bursting point. Ignored so long, your whole body is expectant, like fruit heavy with juice. You are so ready for the hand that picks you, it doesn't even matter whose hand it is.

Every woman has her moment of greatest beauty, that point of fullest bloom, and this was yours. Chris saw it. The little john swooned.

His desire for thrills disappeared. His enthusiasm to try out a cheap Chinese whore turned to adoration. The adoration boys all over the world feel for ripe beautiful women. That age-old, predictable adoration.

Nothing could make him brave now, not even the inferiority everyone of his race ascribed to everyone of yours, including you personally. He could no longer muster his bravado. He just stared at you with those blue eyes, watching you cracking melon seeds with your teeth, watching you pour tea for him. And when you cooled his tea, breath by breath, he trembled with longing.

You look in his eyes now. Stop pretending you don't see the soul floating to the surface of that blue. This marks the beginning of the destiny between you.

After that first time, when he'd left so abruptly after only barely touching your feet, he kept coming back to see you. To watch you play the flute or embroider shoes, to watch you crack melon seeds with your teeth or eat fish heads. Every now and then he opened his mouth too, to ask you something about China, and you just smiled. Sometimes he pulled out a pretty pebble or a beetle that changed colors and reverently placed it in your palm. Each time he came, he stayed just a short time, never more than ten minutes. But each time he left, he frowned and said, Wait for me. A worried look came over his face, funny and moving at the same time.

As if he had forgotten what had brought him to you in the first place, he kept postponing the day he would have you as a man did a woman. He never ate his favorite Swiss chocolate right away either; he always saved it for later. He saved anything he loved from his desire, until he couldn't save it any longer.

You had no idea what he did after he left you. Of course, he had to go back to his own people. He had to pass through the whole city. The city in your day was still in the womb, a strange embryo. But it already had quite a reputation: for prostitutes from all over the world, for gunfights, con games, and high-stakes gambling. Men were routinely kidnapped to work on the ships because the original crews were always running off to the gold mines. Those who had no luck panning for gold were roaming the streets with fake money and real guns and bellies full of hellfire.

You've only been here a month, so you haven't really seen this town called Gold Mountain. You don't know how cruel people can be to men with queues and women with bound feet. As one steamship after another arrives, they can smell the war and famine at your backs. They mutter, Refugee heathens. And as they watch your boundless hordes trudging ashore, they realize something is enormously wrong. You are the most terrible creatures in the world. You're inscrutable. You'll put up with anything. You will humbly and meekly begin overrunning the place.

The same thing happens when we come pouring out the airport gates and people suddenly stare at us so anxiously. Suspicion on both sides elides a hundred years of history and the past shoots right back through us.

It's very hard for me to explain this feeling to you.

Chris has been riding horses since he was seven. Right

now, his horse is following a path along the coast. Not far off a group of men is laughing uproariously. Chris hasn't noticed—people seldom take notice of all the craziness around here. There is a Chinese man in the group, true to type, short and slight, blinking his shifty little eyes, showing his front teeth in his uncertainty. He is shouldering a pole, carrying two baskets of crab he's just caught. This is how he makes his living. A group of white men has blocked his way. They string his queue—the braid all Chinese men wear—over a tree limb, suspending his entire body. He doesn't understand any of their accusations, which include eating anything on earth that walks or swims, wearing a queue, and shouldering a pole. He hangs there in silence, thinking, endure and it will pass. But his mute endurance—his bewildering silence and gentleness—makes them cut off his ears, nose, and tongue. Chris doesn't even notice the tattered body swaying in the wind. He has yet to realize that the infatuation one feels for what one cannot understand is just as violent as the animosity.

His infatuation with you has left him time for nothing else. In his dreams, he is much taller, brandishing a long sword. A knight of courage and passion. An Oriental princess imprisoned in a dark cell waits for him to rescue her. She has dyed her nails red with the juice of pressed blossoms. She has silk for skin. She sticks blood-soaked watermelon seeds one by one between her lips and makes steps of pained grace on the mutilated points of her feet.

Trapped in degradation, the girl plays her tearful bamboo flute and waits for him. The boy is disconsolate; the image in his daydream—the golden female body, partly covered with long black tresses—is you.

Chris isn't thinking about all the hatred fermenting against the Chinese.

His mind is filled with your body laid out across the bamboo bed, waiting to be used to satisfaction. This is the image you have branded upon his whole life.

Don't move. Just lie there and let me take a closer look at the body you use to entertain the whole world.

AMAH WAS TAKING FUSANG to auction. She had already been sold by two other madams.

The whippings had stopped three days ago. Amah told her this was to give her time to heal.

Fusang, you won't even open your mouth to hawk yourself. Why the hell should I keep you? Amah said, her tenderness laced with disdain.

Wiping the chamber pot, Fusang looked up at her.

Just to look at you, Amah continued, no one could tell you're slow. She sighed, trying to figure out how such great beauty and low intellect could combine in one person.

Fusang lowered her head and devoted herself to polishing the pot.

Amah continued listing Fusang's failings as she opened the little cabinet in her room and took out some clothes and a few pieces of costume jewelry. She said, I'm selling you, so you won't be needing these anymore. Fusang, don't you make me cry. You girls I can't keep just make me cry my eyes out.

In the surface of the chamber pot, Fusang saw a distorted Amah lift her shirt to wipe her face, exposing a pale belly rubbed slack by countless men.

Just like the madams before her, Amah opened Fusang's small bundle and inspected each and every item to see whether she'd stolen anything. Picking up a green glass bracelet and trying it out against the color of her own skin, Amah asked, Is this yours or mine? Before Fusang could reply, she said, Never mind. I said all along I'd give it to you. Fusang, you really haven't stolen much at all.

Fusang couldn't recall which of the dead girls had left her the bracelet. Looking at Amah, all she could do was smile.

The auction was held in a basement room that would take five minutes to cross. Fusang had never seen an auction hall so big.

Wooden stools and a teak chair were lined up along one wall. The stools were all taken, but no one was sitting in the chair.

Two madams in their thirties were taking turns massaging each other's necks and shoulders and groaning with satisfaction.

At midnight, a man came down the stairs. He was taller

than most Chinese men, and well built. His queue was incredibly thick. It quickly became apparent why: His hair grew from the nape of his neck down his upper back, like the mane of a horse or lion. His freshly shaven forehead was the color of steel.

Someone shouted, Ah Ding, I haven't seen you in ages!

Me neither, the guy named Ah Ding answered with a laugh, commanding the teak chair and crossing one leg over the other with exaggerated ease. Five daggers, stuck in an elaborately tooled leather sheath at his waist, showed through his open jacket. He wore a ring on every finger, big rings with big colorful stones.

Someone said, Hey, Ah Ding, that wasn't you the vigilantes shot?

He laughed again, How the fuck do I know? Come on up and have a look. He toyed with his gold necklace, which was as thick as a leash. How're the goods? he asked, looking up.

The goods were huddled in one corner, behind several reed curtains that formed a pen.

Someone called, Come out, come on out!

The naked goods filed onto the stage. One girl's cough sounded like a gong.

Ah Ding said, They're just bags of bones, why bother? He chewed on a wad of tobacco.

Fusang was at the back. Unlike the others, she wore shoes and a top that reached her thighs. When Ah Ding saw her, his brow twitched. He thought she was probably somewhat stupid, for her face showed no anxiety or fear, just an earnest smile. She was smiling to herself. Her big black doltish eyes shone. Her face was red and shiny, and three raw scratches, left by sharp fingernails, ran from the corner of her mouth down her neck. The scratches clashed with her gentleness.

Sensing Ah Ding's gaze, Fusang glanced at him, but her eyelids drooped and she blinked. Through and through, she was a broken-in mare.

He took another look at the rounded legs beneath her top, wrapped in an even layer of fat. The fat on her torso was just as well distributed, and jiggled slightly when she grinned or breathed.

Ah Ding said, Tell her to take off her clothes.

She can't, she's filthy, said Amah.

Ah Ding spat out the wad of spent tobacco and said, Who's going to get her to take off that top?

Amah said, She's on the rag, she'll bleed all over the place. She's a real gusher, that one!

Ah Ding laughed and a trace of lewdness crossed his face. The others were familiar with this look. Once the bidding got underway, he pulled a hair from his queue, wound the ends around his index fingers, forced it between his teeth, and sawed back and forth a few times, dislodging flakes of chewing tobacco. He sucked air through the spaces between his teeth and shut his eyes a moment, as if napping, or scheming. The others were familiar with this too.

He opened his eyes and noticed that the thing one of the fifteen-year-olds cradled in her arms wasn't a cloth bundle but a baby girl.

Five months, the auctioneer said.

Not much bigger than a skinned rat, a customer opined.

Look how pretty she is, a perfect oval face, the auctioneer shot back.

What did you pay for her, Third Uncle? A dime? Twenty cents tops!

Twenty cents? Just look at those eyes—they'll be hooking men before she's three!

I'm just afraid, Ah Ding said, that she'll hook my dog and he'll carry her off and chew her up. Straight-faced, he watched everyone else laugh.

It was Fusang's turn. She showed the crowd her open palm, on which her price was inked: one thousand.

Amah stood behind her, lips tight, scanning the crowd.

The auctioneer shouted, Opening at a thousand!

Amah stood on her toes to reach up and swipe Fusang's hair loose and then led her through a turn by the hair clenched in her hand.

The auctioneer shouted, That's real hair!

Someone called out, Eleven hundred!

Amah pried open Fusang's lips to show off the perfect teeth. A man came up and patted Fusang's cheek. Amah said, What are you doing? She doesn't have bad breath!

The man stuck his nose up to Fusang's open mouth and said, I wouldn't quite call it good.

The auctioneer shouted, Do I hear fifteen?

Amah pulled off one of Fusang's shoes and walked the crowd with it displayed in her palm, saying, These genuine four-inch golden lotuses are really three-point-eight.

A madam in her thirties, a melon seed shell flying from her mouth, asked, If she's so great, why are you selling her?

You don't know? the madam sitting beside her said. She won't hawk herself. She can't even earn her keep. Forget about her size, she hasn't got a nickel's worth of brains!

Eleven hundred fifty!

Twelve hundred!

Ah Ding stopped swinging his crossed leg and asked, Amah Mei, how old is she?

She's twenty and she's a virgin, Amah replied.

Twenty? Ah Ding chuckled. If she's still a virgin, she's probably rusted shut.

Amah said, Ah Ding, a thousand lashes!

Ah Ding, still chuckling, raised a hand and bid, Nine fifty.

Amah looked at Ah Ding, then looked at the auctioneer and whined, This girl's from the inland! Pointing at the brood of naked bodies, she continued, Not like these port and delta girls! How many foreign sailors on the docks? You think any of these girls is still clean? This girl's different, she's inland, and if I say she's a virgin, then she's a virgin!

Ah Ding said, Nine hundred. To the dumbstruck faces around him, he repeated, Nine hundred!

The auctioneer scratched his chin and shouted, Twelve hundred! An inland girl, from a good home! She cooks, she embroiders, and she plays the flute! Twelve hundred!

Ah Ding said, Eight fifty. He licked his lips. They were big and thick; every smile burst open his face for a long time before finally seeping down to his mouth.

Everyone looked away. All the brothels had lost a girl or two and it was common knowledge they had been stolen. Yet no one dared accuse Ah Ding. No one around here wanted to offend him; he had a couple of dozen hatchet men at his command and all he had to do was whistle and they'd come running. And his reputation wasn't confined to Chinatown—whites had heard the stories about him too. It was said that the time forty Chinese men had their queues cut off, slashes appeared on the backs of a hundred whites the next day. The knives had cut through coats, vests, and shirts, but never once broke skin. It was as if on the way to stabbing they had suddenly decided against it.

Ah Ding pulled out his purse and began counting out his money.

Pouting, Amah watched him. The stolen girls would reappear in little towns near the gold mines, but no one ever managed to pin anything on Ah Ding. His numerous enterprises included both the illegal and the legal—loan-sharking, an aphrodisiac factory, shipping tons of dirty clothes back to China to be laundered. But they did not include speculation in women. The stealing and selling of prostitutes was strictly entertainment for him, a diversion for his mischievous streak. As Ah Ding was counting out his money for the third time, the lookout came in and said the cops were coming, and they'd already blocked off the streets.

A painting on the wall was torn down and the panels behind it pried free to uncover the secret passage.

Someone yelled to the naked girls, Get dressed, quick!

Ah Ding said, No, if they're naked, they won't run off on us. He wound his queue onto the top of his head.

The secret passage was only as wide as a square table for eight and six tables long, and everyone was pressing in, skin to skin. Ah Ding was the last to squeeze in. He said to the girls, who were so scared their teeth were chattering, Anyone makes a sound and I'll strangle her. The ceiling reverberated with the clomping of riding boots.

If the four men staging a mahjong game didn't fool the police, the search and ransack would begin. The police knew these auctions usually had a secret passage and they would knock across every inch of the floor and walls until they found it.

Fusang was cradling the bundle—someone had shoved it into her arms in the commotion. The whole building shook with the stomping of boots. The baby burst into wails.

Everyone stopped breathing, lest they add the slightest sound or motion to the place.

Cover its mouth, someone said.

A hand did so, and Fusang could feel the little thing squirming. The owner of the hand crooned, Little ancestor, little ancestor . . .

But the wailing kept escaping.

The boots came clomping down the stairs.

Ah Ding said, Give me the worthless little wench. His tone was gentle as he crowded his way toward the crying, stepping on the big feet of the men and the little feet of the women.

Don't be too rough, Ah Ding.

Who, me? No way.

Ah Ding, what the hell are you doing?

The group pressed inward, becoming a single slab of flesh.

Again Ah Ding said, Anyone who makes a sound I strangle. His tone remained as gentle as before.

His hand cupped the little head precisely, like palming a piece of fruit. Then he pulled it free from the swaddling, his other hand already on the baby's neck. The crying weakened and stopped. The group twitched, then became a slab of dead flesh again.

The boots had reached the basement.

Fusang's feet ached and she wanted to shift her step,

but couldn't move, for the tiny corpse was piled still warm at her feet. Standing on the other side of it was Ah Ding.

He pulled a match from his pocket, struck it, and bent down to examine the life he'd just taken. He sighed with satisfaction, then lifted the flame to Fusang's bare leg and raised it all the way up to her face.

The image of Ah Ding flickered behind the flame. Fusang couldn't figure out what he was doing. No one ever knew what it meant when Ah Ding arched an eyebrow.

The match burned down to his fingers, then burned a moment longer before it went out.

YOU LOWER YOUR HEAD AND WATCH those ring-covered fingers pinching the flame shining on the dead little face.

The five-month-old eyes stare at him as if still alive. The little creature is memorizing the handsome face of the man who took her life. Two new baby teeth show between her tiny lips.

Your leg trembles and you want to pull your foot out from under the tiny sacrifice growing heavier and colder there. You realize that the little thing will remember not just Ah Ding but all of you, because when she started crying, every single one of you would have sacrificed her innocent life to preserve your own. Ah Ding was simply the one who acted on everyone's secret wish. In a sense, all of you borrowed Ah Ding's hands to stop it, to kill it, to put a halt to its unwitting betrayal of you.

Don't deny it: Every people must ensure its survival,

and so there will always be sacrifices and offerings, times when they kill their own. Of course you couldn't have been conscious of that secret desire. Ah Ding, however, understood the intimacy of killing one's own.

But it's too late—the clomping of the policemen's boots is getting louder. A traitor had already led them to this underground female slave auction. Ah Ding had strangled the baby hard enough to kill the real traitor. Ah Ding never let off anyone who betrayed his own.

With an expression as innocent as the baby girl's, you ask me about Ah Ding. Wait a minute while I find a description of him in this pile of histories. Well, it looks like that was wishful thinking. The books talk about dozens of Chinatown kingpins, but only as stereotypes. Ah Ding has been omitted entirely. I can bring him to light though. I am the only one who can give you a clear picture of this good-looking man with the mane. He has the beauty of an animal. When you saw him examining you from behind the flame, he looked just like a panther.

As the match crept steadily up your leg, you noticed his face illuminated by the flame. You couldn't interpret the infatuation in his arched eyebrow. The same infatuation clutches him when he comes across a find in a dark pawn shop.

When the flame licked your face, you smiled. You didn't duck away. You knew it was no use. Escape was out of the question for you, just as it was for the baby. Your smile was the sudden, unconscious, simpleminded smile of a lamb at slaughter.

To me, your smile took on the slack-jawed, glassy-eyed expression of the dead baby.

Unfortunately, Ah Ding thought your smile was meant for him.

The rings on his fingers could split skin during a fist-fight. You saw the metallic sheen of his forehead and his queue coiled like an ancient vine.

And you saw all the murders on his hands.

You didn't know what he was looking at as the tromping of the policemen's boots came closer. Maybe the way your feet seemed too small for your body? Perhaps he thought the same things about Chinese prostitutes as foreign johns, who wrote in their books: "Their deformed feet and unique gait influence the development of their bodies in many significant ways, one of which is the abnormally crooked pelvic and vaginal cavities. This is where the mystique of the Oriental woman is to be found. Just as this race excels at the art of potted landscape, these deformed female bodies offer an enjoyment that defies description."

As Ah Ding lifted the flame to your face, he seemed obsessed by the proportion between your feet and body, oblivious to the fact that the police were at that very moment turning the place out.

THE NEWS OF THE NIGHT RAID on the underground auction on Jackson Street made the morning papers.

It was said the police first arrived on horseback, but found only four men playing mahjong and two others singing Cantonese opera. The police went to the corner, tethered their horses, and then came back and surrounded the place on foot. When they broke down the door, half of the two dozen people had just emerged from the hidden passage.

It was said that the mahjong players put out all the lights, so the police had to check their flintlocks and switch to nightsticks.

It was said that Ah Ding single-handedly held the police at bay while everyone else got away through the doors and routes they knew so well.

It was said that Ah Ding didn't throw a single dagger, but ended up breaking two rings punching cops. He came running out at four in the morning with his queue clamped between his teeth, a cop missing an eye hot on his heels. Chased to the coast, Ah Ding, who had already taken a couple of bullets, turned to face the cop and opened his jacket. As soon as the cop saw the daggers, he knew who this was. So many stories of the gangster with the daggers had circulated among whites that he may as well have been the devil. The daggers were supposedly dipped in poison, a secret potion three thousand years old. In short, the cop flung himself to the ground, and by the time he crawled up, Ah Ding had jumped into the sea and disappeared.

It was said that Ah Ding was good at jumping into the sea and disappearing. And each and every time, he would resurface on the streets three months later.

But not this time. Three months passed, and he wasn't standing at the counter of Daiji pawnshop redeeming his emerald pocket watch. Nor was he lounging on a chaise at Chan bathhouse having his foot-long black mane washed, or leaning in the doorway of Zhangji's fish market, his Stetson pulled low, gulping down a bowl of water full of thrashing tadpoles. Every other time, invariably someone would bow to him and say, So, Ah Ding, you're back.

Ah Ding would snarl, Whaddya mean, back? Wasn't I sleeping with your wife just last night?

Soon he was ancient history in a city that grew as fast as cancer and came up with tall tales daily.

Only the prostitutes who bought his picture could prove he'd ever been here at all. At the age of seventeen, Ah Ding began printing nude photos of himself to sell to hookers. The first buyers were South American and Polish and then gradually the Chinese. He never got more than seventy cents for them and never sold them himself; he had vendors of hair oil, ribbons, and chignon blossoms peddle them up and down the streets. While he wasn't the most handsome man around, his amazing ability to be offensive matched the evil of the city notorious for it. The hookers bought his photo for its magical powers, to use evil to ward off evil.

By the third year, no one even remembered to wonder whether Ah Ding would return or not. The little baby girl he'd strangled to death had become a mound of earth. The little teeth that had once vaguely entertained the notion of biting someone were now chewing on the roots of spring flowers and autumn grasses. The foreign histories a hundred years later barely mentioned her at all: "The youngest of the Chinese girls sold into prostitution here was five months old."

One day, two whites came to Chinatown, barged into the fruit shop, the jeweler's, and the pedicurist's, and forced the cashiers to hand over the money through the slot in the wire mesh. Their last stop was the herbalist's, where they set piles of medicinal roots and bark on fire. People finally believed that Ah Ding and his daggers were no more.

With Ah Ding gone, whites routinely strolled in and out of shops and took the cash.

Most of the girls who escaped the police roundup that night were dead by now, killed by disease, by a fight, by who knows what.

Fusang was the one who didn't die.

Fusang, who in two years had aborted five pregnancies with caustic drugs, had a rounder face now. She went out around noon with Ah Cha and Ah Jiao to buy a few feet of satin to make embroidered shoe tops.

The three women walked in front, and a thug followed a few paces behind, to make sure they didn't run off. Once the women's pace quickened, he hopped on his horse. When the streets got crowded, he stayed on horseback to keep an eye on the women's every intention, however minor it might be.

The women stopped at a fruit stand to buy slices of pineapple, and then bought pouches of fried river snails and barbecued duck livers at a food stand. They didn't pay for any of it. Thanking the vendors, they walked off eating and the thug came behind and settled up.

As they passed Chan bathhouse, the women slowed down. A few hundred men were going in one door and coming out another. When they went in they were heavier and darker and when they came out they were thinner, their faces lighter. The men going in the front door undressed and handed their clothes to an attendant, who took them to a pawnshop. He stopped and bought new clothes on his way back, returning just in time to give them to the men as they climbed out of the water.

Rid of lice, beard, tartar, and long finger- and toenails, the men coming out the back door of the bathhouse gave off warm steam, as if they had just been blanched. Brothel madams always checked the men's nails; they had to be clipped to the nub and filed smooth so the girls weren't left covered with scratches by the end of the night.

Ah Cha said, That guy of mine is probably here.

How many guys you got? Ah Jiao asked, slapping her on the bottom.

Just one, not like you! Ah Cha said. When he's made enough money he's gonna come for me.

Ah Jiao said, They all say that. She tossed an empty snail shell over her shoulder, hitting Ah Cha in the chest. Laughing and squealing, the two of them chased and slapped and cursed each other, attracting the attention of the men waiting outside the bathhouse.

Hey Fusang, what about you? Ah Cha asked. How many guys you got out there?

Fusang shook her head and laughed. She was wearing a peach-pink blouse and wide-legged pants of black gauze. As Fusang knelt down to pull up her shoe, Ah Jiao whispered in Ah Cha's ear, Who could she have? She can't even remember their names! Look at her; she turns as rosy as pork lungs at the mere sight of so many men.. . .Ah Jiao stopped, stifling her laughter with her hand.

The men outside the bathhouse watched them hungrily.

Hey, which house are you from? Another shouted, I'll be over to see you later!

Her lips suddenly moist, Fusang stood up and gave them a smile.

Another yelled, I've got a bar of foreign soap, it sure smells nice. I'll save you half!

The thug hurried them along.

A crowd circled an Indian snake charmer.

Another crowd was gathered around two Chinese men putting on a meat chopping performance. Fusang craned her neck to get a better look. She was taller than her two companions, who kept asking her what was going on. One guy was kneeling on the ground, his back serving as a cutting board on which the other guy was mincing a hunk of beef. At the end of the act, the kneeling man's back was completely unscathed.

Ah Jiao exclaimed, That's not necessarily beef!

Ah Cha said, Then what is it?

Ah Jiao replied with a mischievous smile, One day someone disappears, the next day it's someone else— where do they go? When have you ever seen cattle around here?

The three women burst into peals of laughter. Three pairs of tiny feet in red embroidered shoes kicked up little clumps of dirt as they ran into the street. A horse and buggy was coming, and the women stopped to get out of the way, patting their chests and panting.

A distinguished white devil in his fifties stuck his head out the gauze curtain of the coach.

Hey, you Chinese hookers, get out of the way!

They grabbed one another's hands. We have, one said.

Go hide in that doorway until my carriage has passed! My wife and daughter are inside, get it?

With a flurry of little feet, the three of them retreated inside the teahouse. They understood: Proper white devil women shouldn't lay eyes on girls like them. They were permitted to exist, but not in the same time and place as the women in the carriage. They were supposed to leave the world clean for such women.

Ah Jiao and Ah Cha wanted to continue their walk; Fusang said she'd wait for them in the teahouse. The thug went to tail the other two, knowing he wouldn't have to worry much about Fusang. One time Fusang ran off with another girl without even really knowing what she was doing and came back on her own the very next day.

When they tried to beat an explanation out of her, she just smiled and replied slowly, Yesterday I ran away and today I ran back. Fusang's obedience was just part of her simple streak.

The wind dispersed the fog and the sun slanted through the teahouse doorway.

Gently as a worm, Fusang inched into the sunlight.

Business was slow at Chan Teahouse—two men sitting across the room. They were greengrocers who made deliveries to restaurants before daybreak, shouldering baskets of vegetables on their carrying poles. Now their poles leant against their legs and a few leftover bunches of greens drooped like their faces—this would be their dinner.

They watched Fusang and whispered like crickets.

Then the waiter came over and said, The two gentlemen want to know if you'd like a little business on your time off.

She looked past his shoulder and greeted them with her eyes.

The waiter winked at the grocers and said to her, Pick up a little business while you're here and you won't have to give the money to your amah. Just slip me some extra change for the tea and we'll call it even. Come on now, lift your head, let them see you. He pointed to the back of the room, which was hidden in shadow, and added, We've got an opium den back there with no customers right now. He got straight to the point: Look, you're not doing anything anyway.

She looked at the two cabbage yellow faces again and gave them a big smile. Torn, she shook her head and said, I'm just taking it easy before I go.

The waiter was just about to try again when another customer walked in, a little white devil in his teens. His riding boots were covered with dust, but his white shirt and pants were spotless. He wore a blue cloak draped over his shoulders and a riding cap, his blond hair visible under the brim. He could have walked right out of an illustration in a book. The dingy Chinese teahouse suddenly formed a most absurd backdrop for him.

He noticed Fusang as he headed toward a table and abruptly turned and approached her.

She drew in her hands and feet. Languor from the sunlight weighed upon her body. She tried to think. Who is this little white devil? She looked at him as if she was struggling to extricate herself from a dream.

He froze at his sudden luck. He'd been looking for her for two years. He'd never stopped looking for her. His memory of her was so intense it had become a void that nothing else could fill. Now he realized she was even stranger than the woman he'd seen at twelve. The peach-pink of her silk blouse bled into the drabness around her.

As she watched him sit down, she tried not to keep thinking, Who *is* this little white devil?

Do you still remember me? Chris asked her. All the johns asked this; all of them hoped like this.

She said, Mmm.

He stared at her intently as he took off his cap. Now

he was almost a head taller than she was, as tall as a grown man. His limbs were long and lanky and all his joints seemed oversized. He had the neck of a child, but the Adam's apple of a man. He put his elbows on the table, noticed the filth, and pulled them back. He was as flustered as a child.

I looked for you, he said. His voice was still changing and cracked with awkwardness.

My name is Chris, he continued.

Chris, she repeated with a smile.

He smiled back and said, You still say my name that same cute way.

Remembering suddenly, Fusang said, You comed with your uncle. She said this twice in a row. Like all Chinese prostitutes, she spoke English like a two-year-old, with cute little syllables at the ends of words.

He winced and shook his head, his hurt laced with the affront of being mistaken for someone he wasn't by a grown-up.

Fusang said, I'm sorry.

Never mind.

I really am sorry, Fusang said again, consoling him with her eyes.

It doesn't matter. He frowned and looked away. He hated the way adults could be so insensitive.

The grocers walked over, carrying their poles and baskets. They looked at him, then at her, and then one of them said, You want us to break his kneecaps for you?

When Chris turned to see what they were saying, they bobbed their heads a couple of times in greeting.

No need today, Fusang said to them with a smile. Thank you, elder brothers.

My shop's just across the street; if the little white devil gives you a hard time, I'll come back with a cleaver, no problem.

There's no need; he hasn't done anything wrong.

If he gives you any trouble, just call. I'll take him out at the knees, no big deal.

Thank you.

My pleasure.

With a final nod at Chris, they walked out the door, straightening their hats.

Fusang stood too, straightened her shirt, and said to Chris, It's getting late.

The waiter came over to tell her the grocers had paid for her tea. Motioning toward Chris, he said, There's nothing I can do. I can't kick him out. The white devils waltz in here like Chinatown is the outhouse in their own backyard.

Fusang glanced at Chris in farewell and stepped over the high threshold. Across the street, a crowd was watching the grand opening of a variety meats shop. The foreigners were cringing at the noise of firecrackers. Two female impersonators on stilts were holding a crock of marinade from China, an old Ming dynasty recipe. Several strings of firecrackers went off at once, exploding debris everywhere. The shopkeeper and clerks ushered the crock inside as if it were one of their own ancestors.

Fusang squeezed through the crowd. Looking back almost unconsciously, she saw Chris five or six paces behind her.

When she stopped, he did too. He looked like a waif standing there in the wind. His persistence disrupted her sluggish thoughts. She knew she'd never forgotten the boy.

She was surprised to find him quite handsome.

She stood there locking eyes with him. She had never held eyes so long with anyone. The firecrackers down the street were exploding at the tip of every hair on her body, at the tips of her eyelashes.

Finally, she lowered her eyes, but he did not.

ONE HUNDRED AND TWENTY-EIGHT YEARS AGO, you and he stood where I am now. The ground is still covered with the red debris of firecrackers, but bubble gum has replaced the phlegm. White cops have been fining Chinese for spitting for a good seventy or eighty years now. You see? The gum, which doesn't evaporate, represents progress.

You and Chris are standing here. The variety meats shop on the left has changed storefronts dozens of times by now, and the right side of the street has changed even more. With all the fires and earthquakes, historians lost track of all the changes over the years. Yet the moment when you and Chris stand here locking eyes is an undocumented eternity. The trembling brought on by such a gaze continues to this day. I don't know how many times my husband and I have trembled when my eyes meet the gray depths of his—in the infatuation born of our differences, in our desire to understand each other, it stops mattering how close we are; trembling, we become strangers to each other.

Awareness returns with a single breath. You are aware of your strange feet, the high collar tight around your neck, your cold faux jade bracelet. You are aware of the heartbeat of every embroidered blossom on your peach silk blouse. You know this boy named Chris wants something other than your body.

But you don't know why he got on his horse and rode into the city from his father's estate first thing that morning. He'd followed the lily white crowd—eighty thousand strong—thronging the municipal government to protest Chinese coolies, opium addicts, and prostitutes. At first Chris just wanted a look. But the excitement was contagious and soon he was picking up handbills from the ground, dusting them off, and handing them out to bewildered passersby.

Even now his pocket contains one of those handbills. It lists over ten accusations against the Chinese: "The men wear queues, the women bind their feet, their diet consists primarily of vegetables and rice, they live in crowded unsanitary quarters, they spread TB, they hoard their wages for use in their native land. . . ." It suggests that such an evil, inferior race ought to be wiped out. He thinks of you. He certainly doesn't want you wiped out; instead, he wishes everything around you would be, leaving only you behind. He doesn't know that everything he wants to wipe out is precisely what gives you your appeal, your opiumlike powers.

Chris looks at you with the eyes of an addict.

ONCE UPON A TIME, there was a mountain in China called Tea Mountain, and on that mountain lived a few dozen families of tea growers. They planted tea, they picked tea, they sang Tea Mountain songs—this was the life of a few dozen families, generation after generation. You couldn't call them happy, yet you wouldn't say they suffered either. There was no evil landlord; when the two rich families slaughtered pigs, they always gave a chunk of lard to every household.

Halfway up the mountain lived a family neither poor nor rich, who had enough to eat, whose clothes were patched with no more than two colors. Their fourth daughter was born on the road to Changsha, and the tea buyer there chose a name for her, Fusang.

Fusang was engaged while still in the cradle to an eight-year-old young master from Guangdong. The next year, the young master crossed the ocean to Gold Mountain with some of his uncles in search of gold. Every few years, Fusang received yard goods for clothing or colorful hair ribbons, with word that Young Master had sent them back across the sea for her.

Someone from Young Master's family came two or three times to see Fusang and was pleased to find her slow of mind and speech. Once she married in, they could treat her like chattel and she wouldn't say a word. One time they gave her a silver bracelet and said it was from Young Master too.

And then one year the youth's uncles came back bearing gold, saying Young Master wanted to marry right away. Fusang was fourteen.

After traveling rivers and roads, she arrived at her mother-in-law's to find a big red rooster tied to a post, ready, as custom mandated, to stand in for the absent groom. Fusang and the rooster were hurried into the hall; someone grabbed Fusang's head, someone else grabbed the rooster's, and after who knows how many kowtows they'd paid their respects to the whole room. From beneath her veil, Fusang could see the rooster staring at her with its yellow eyes, rubbing its beak back and forth on the ground as if sharpening a knife.

When they entered the bridal chamber, the sun had just moved west. The rooster was put under the bed and Fusang was placed upon it. She fell asleep and slept straight through until morning, when she discovered the rooster lying dead and stiff beside her pillow.

After that, she never received yard goods or hair ribbons from Young Master again.

A few years later, Fusang ran into a stranger on her way to market.

He said, I've come back across the sea; your husband asked me to bring you over to him so you two can be a real married couple. Will you come?

Fusang shook her head.

Come on, your in-laws use you to farm, to cook, to chop pig feed—your mother-in-law has married you in for herself. Don't you know that?

Fusang said she knew.

If you don't come now, you'll never see your husband again for the rest of your life! Without a husband, you can't have kids, and how'll you get a daughter-in-law to cook and do laundry for you in your old age?

Fusang said nothing, just returned with a smile to the bamboo hat she was weaving.

Here's a boat ticket—your husband bought it for you. Will you get on the boat with me?

Is it far?

No, no, not far at all. It's right on the other side of the sea.

Okay, just let me run home and tell them, grab a couple sweet potatoes, and the eight pairs of shoes I made for him . . .

No time! The boat's leaving right now! Your husband wears shoes of calfskin, sheepskin, shoes made of skins of sharks from the sea—the price of one pair alone is enough to buy half a *mu* of paddy land!

I should bring my box of hair things though, shouldn't I?

Across the sea, they've got wide-toothed combs of gold and fine-toothed combs of silver! What more could you want?

Fusang left with the man with the greasy hair.

They passed a food stall where a neighbor sat on a rattan chair eating rice noodles. She called out, Fusang, where're you going?

My husband sent for me. That hand loom I borrowed from you yesterday—if I don't get a chance to return it in a day or two, go ask my mother-in-law for it.

Holding her bowl in both hands, the neighbor leapt out of her chair to see Fusang held fast at the sleeve by the man, her pointy little feet quick as spindles.

When the man settled Fusang on the boat, a woman heating a poultice on a little brazier in the bow struck up a friendly conversation with her. She pulled out a strip of cloth and tied her own ankles together, and when Fusang asked her why, she explained that women crossing the sea weren't allowed to have two legs; it was a violation of ocean law and the boat would sink. So Fusang followed her example and tied herself up too.

The man closed the curtain and the boat began to move. Fusang heard her neighbor shout from the bank, Fusang! Get off that boat!

Unable to move, Fusang shouted back from behind the curtain.

Sculling rapidly, the man said, What're you calling, a cat or a dog?

The neighbor said, I'm calling the one who just answered me. Fusang, return my hand loom before you go! Fusang!

From behind the bamboo curtain, Fusang could see her neighbor running frantically back and forth, yelling at her through hands cupped around her mouth like a horn. The stretch of water between the boat and shore began to widen.

The neighbor suddenly turned and looked around, shouting, Help! Somebody! Kidnappers again! They've kidnapped Fusang! Fusang, you answer me!

Fusang had no sooner opened her mouth to shout back than the woman on the boat jumped up and whipped off the tie binding her ankles. She leaned into the bow and came back palming the poultice, baked to a pulp. Before Fusang could shout much of anything, the woman pasted her mouth shut with the hot dripping poultice.

When the woman came back later that night to remove it, she smiled with a sigh and urged Fusang not to take it all to heart, to have a bite to eat; besides, all the knives and scissors and ropes on the boat were hidden away—suicide would be no easy task.

Her mouth smeared with black gunk, Fusang took the bowl of congee and slurped it down.

The woman couldn't believe it. Of all the kidnapped girls, Fusang was the only one who didn't raise a huge fuss and refuse to eat.

Fusang was put onto a big ship. The hold was packed with girls. The first day, one of them got boils; the next day every last one of them had the very same boils. They were like a pile of sweet potatoes, each rotting in concert with the others.

Fusang was the only one sitting up. Even sitting, she could sleep soundly, completely unaware of the two guys who came in each night to take the girls whose color and odor had changed and throw them overboard.

Gradually, the space in the hold grew larger. When she opened her eyes each morning, Fusang couldn't even remember who was missing.

One day someone shouted, We made it! We're there! That big lighthouse is Gold Mountain City!

It had taken three months.

The middleman went down to the hold, counted the girls with his finger, then counted again in disbelief, and said, Fuck!

Stand up, stand up straight! Shut your eyes tight!

Armed with a big cake of powder and another of rouge, he dabbed a big brush first in white and then in red, and brushed the girls' faces up and down, back and forth. Each rosy face was stuck atop a dark thin neck, marionettes all of them.

Fusang closed her eyes too, waiting for him to brush her face, but he didn't. He decided she wasn't worth the waste of his powder and rouge.

He yelled, Each of you hold on to the clothes of the next! No looking around! No smiling at anybody! There's no people here, only devils! White devils, black devils, red Indian devils!

Once ashore, they saw the Customs devils. There were three of them in all, and a furry black creature, taller than the table, which no one quite believed was a dog.

A bald Chinese man greeted them with glee, Come over here, I'm your father. He turned to the Customs devil with the big beard and said, These are my five daughters.

A young Customs devil pushed him back into a stagger, Take one more step and I'll sic this dog on you.

Baldy repeated to the girls, Remember, I'm your father! Your mother's dead!

The young devil dropped the leash, and the dog-shaped creature lunged. Baldy scurried backward and quickly instructed the girls, Your mother starved to death. Don't say she died of illness or the Customs devils will lock you up for inspection!

Half an hour later, the Chinese translator arrived. He knew better than to translate everything accurately, or there would be nothing left of him by morning.

Ask her, Big Beard Devil said, pointing at Fusang, what her mother's name is.

She says her mother's dead.

I'm asking her mother's name.

She's dead. *Ta si le.*

You shameless lying Chinese!

Fusang had no idea what Big Beard was so mad about.

She smiled amiably, smelling last night's booze on his breath.

If your elder sister can't remember your mother's name, surely you remember. Come on, tell me.

She's dead. *Ta si le*.

Fine. Terrific. And you? Big Beard came to the youngest girl. She was nine at most, shaking from the inside out, as if to rid herself of all her lice and fleas.

You don't know how to lie, my little angel, so please tell me your mother's name.

All activity on the dock stopped, waiting on the nine-year-old girl who was wearing herself out trembling.

She. . .she starved to death. *Ta si le*.

The tip of his tongue protruding, Big Beard said, *Ta si le, ta si le,* just like an enormous parrot reveling over its latest accomplishment in mimicry. This I understand, he said, every last one of you Chinese says it: *ta si le, ta si le*. You lying devils.

Big Beard directed the five girls into three groups with his hand, and said, Think it over, figure out your mother's name. Do your best to prevent your poor unfortunate mother from having too many names.

Baldy, standing a hundred yards away, fell to the ground with a thud, wailing, Oh my wife, my poor wife.

Shut him up, Big Beard said to the translator, who stood there fidgeting.

Baldy continued to wail as he beckoned to the girls with his eyes. What good's it gonna do, standing over there doing nothing? Get over here! Hug me, call me Dad! All at once the girls understood and flung themselves upon him.

Baldy lay there on the ground, taking in the scene. The devils had already acknowledged defeat.

THAT NIGHT, THE BALD MAN called Third Uncle took the girls to a still, where he let them use the hot distillery water to wash off. Third Uncle dealt exclusively in girls. Though lacking in virtue, he was known to be good-natured.

When the baths were finished, Third Uncle brought in two men and a big steelyard. He hung the steelyard from a sturdy carrying pole, and one by one the girls held on to its hook with both hands and curled up their legs. When Third Uncle shouted lift!, the men raised the pole to their shoulders, and the girls became hanging slabs of meat. Holding a lantern in one hand and sliding the weight with the other, Third Uncle shouted, Only fifty catties! Only sixty catties! Fuck your mother, you're lighter than a chicken, you're nothing but a feather duster!

Fusang was the last to be weighed.

When Third Uncle started sliding the weight, he stopped cursing. Finally, he exclaimed, One hundred on the nose!

He told Fusang not to move as he circled her a couple of times, pinching her from head to toe.

She held on with all her might, her legs drawn up like

a snared rabbit, waiting for Third Uncle to finish his inspection.

What did you eat on the ship? he asked.

Sweet potatoes.

He pinched her thigh, looking at her with furrowed brow and a smile. Just sweet potatoes? No meat?

Panting with the effort of hanging there, Fusang said, Just sweet potatoes.

Third Uncle said to the men holding the steelyard, She says she didn't have any meat? Looks like she must've polished off at least two girls on the way over.

The men put Fusang down. One moved in for a better look.

What're you looking at? You can't afford her, so why bother? Third Uncle tied the girls one to the next with a rope.

The other man moved in too, looking into Fusang's eyes as if spying into a dark room through the key hole. He said, You sure she's not dimwitted? She's got the eyes of a zombie.

The first guy said, Third Uncle, how much to have her as my wife for two nights?

She wouldn't be worth a fart after being with you! Nothing but damaged goods, Third Uncle groused cheerfully.

Tying Fusang last, Third Uncle said, If your old uncle could get by without selling you, I'd make all of you my wives.

How did you end up with her, Third Uncle? The man was still reckoning over Fusang.

How did I get her? I stole her, I drugged her, I coaxed her with honeyed words, Third Uncle replied.

Fusang and the other girls were stuffed into a carriage. The coach contained other things too and smelled like salted fish.

The girls cheered up when they realized they'd be eating fish from now on.

When the carriage came to a stop, Third Uncle called for men to come unload the cargo. He pulled a price list from his pocket and handed it to the madam waiting in the doorway. Chinatown's official commodity exchange printed the going rates daily.

The madam took the list under the light to read it.

April 16

rice	$2.00 per sack
fresh shrimp	$.10 per pound
salt fish	$.08 per pound
...	
girls	$6.00 per pound

Holding the list between her fingers, she checked the girls over for scars, ringworm, rot, and blindness. Satisfied, she counted out the money and gave it to Third Uncle.

Be good now, okay? Third Uncle laughed heartily. I'll come see you soon, okay?

SOUND ASLEEP, FUSANG WAS AWAKENED at dawn by a woman's scream, sharp and brittle, like a hog's at slaughter.

Fusang ran into the hall. The four girls who had come with her were already huddled at the door of the next room, looking through the crack.

A woman was lying on the bed, her long black hair loose. She was completely naked, her legs held apart by two men, her wrists tied to the headboard.

A madam was standing at her crotch, holding a short metal skewer with a steady hand.

The screaming was so loud no one noticed the door open.

The woman screamed, Fuck your mother!

Good, said the madam, Keep it up! Louder! If you don't curse the men who gave you the clap, who can you curse? She took up another red hot skewer. Go on, yell louder! What do you have to be ashamed of? Add names to those curses! A wisp of dark smoke rose before the madam's face.

The woman stopped in midscream. Okay, said the madam, catching her breath, it's all over.

The people in the room noticed the girls at the door.

Still gripping the skewer, the madam said to them, We weren't killing her, we were curing her. Go back to bed. Don't get your eyes poked out.

A few days later, Fusang saw the woman come out from

behind the door that had stayed closed the whole time. She nodded and smiled at everyone, and said she was better. She was so thin that when she walked into the sunlight, it shone right through her. She barely cast a shadow. In a strong wind, her thin form curled like a leaf.

She nodded to Fusang.

You new?

Fusang smiled.

She smiled too, showing the ruins behind her four front teeth. She was missing so many teeth that her cheeks formed caves that became enormous dimples when she smiled.

How old are you? she asked Fusang.

Twenty.

Wow, you're old. I'm a year younger than you, and I'm nothing but skin and bones! She laughed.

A few days after that she was gone. She hadn't been seriously ill; the hot skewer treatment had cured her little bout of the clap. She had simply died of old age at the end of a normal life span.

The madam's big round face remained impassive. For better or worse she had done her job raising the girl to old age and seeing her to the grave.

NO MATTER HOW PEOPLE COMPLAINED, or raised their fists, or wrote Chinamen Must Go, the Chinese just kept coming.

Slowly and silently, they came ashore, looking at you

without speaking. If you blocked their way on the right, they would pass on your left, and if you blocked their way entirely, they would bow their heads and patiently wait for you to get out of the way. And sure enough, their patience would end up making you leave.

They spread everywhere, so softly and endlessly—all those steady dark and gentle eyes.

No one had ever seen anything like them.

Hordes of short little bodies trailing queues climbed ashore, and those dark eyes that could endure anything forced you to yield.

For all their docility, they brought in hundreds upon thousands of slave girls. They were gentle with these girls—every last one of them headed for death, throwing countless corpses into the sea with perfect equanimity. The gentleness of these men made cruelty and evil impossible to explain or define. Delivered with such gentleness, cruelty and evil became as incomprehensible as the nonfeet of the women, as strange and unreal as an opium dream.

And as the Chinese enslaved and killed one another in perfect harmony, their numbers grew ever larger and stronger.

Bowing, they invite you into the opium den, its walls painted black with smoke. Make you lose yourself in the darkness. Make the drunken violence in you dissipate. Make smoking daily separate you from your society. Make you stop hating them, murdering them, driving them out; make you lose all natural morality without even wondering why.

You say, Opium is far worse than alcohol.

They just smile and reply, Alcohol makes you destructive; opium makes you tolerate destruction.

When the city itself was still taking shape, they staked out their own little stronghold there, a sink of iniquity, where they produced and consumed all manner of sin in a cycle impervious to reason.

Their way of life was a mystery.

They mystified all standards of good and evil.

The people here had never been so perplexed over a way of life. No standards of culture or morality could ever apply to it.

The people here were terrified of the obscure terrain between gentleness and cruelty.

Handbills scattered from the sky, and one landed right next to the exquisite feet of a Chinese prostitute. How could such righteous indignation and these feet in pink satin relate? Which was mocking the other?

Chris was reluctant to turn and go. He wanted to smile, to loosen up and flirt with Fusang, but he couldn't.

A red door, paint chipping, four silk lanterns hanging above. Nearly every Chinese brothel doorway looks the same, the classy ones ornate, the cheap ones, like the one he has entered, just gaudy.

The music is insistent, the dulcimer hammered like shoe nails, the two-stringed fiddle sawed like a dull knife through meat. The music adds twists and turns to the straight hallway. The whores deftly set their lips in motion, taking in a steady supply of melon seeds on one side of their mouths, spitting split shells from the other.

For two years, Chris charged through one identical Chinese brothel door after another in search of that one-of-a-kind whore.

He never found a single Chinese girl who cracked melon seeds the way Fusang did, who pursed her lips that way, the space between her eyebrows quivering ever so slightly with the crack of each shell, as if breaking open a tiny anguish. Then she shifted her tongue in a manner at once carefree and fraught with care, bringing out the bright red shells, which lingered on her lips for a moment before falling into the saucer. These little clickings of lips and teeth made reticence itself a subtle mode of expression.

He looked for her for two whole years. His desperate search for her, his desire to rescue her, led him time and again to join the mobs against the Chinese.

At fourteen, when he had found her at last, he kept saying, I tried to find you.

She didn't look back at him again.

Chris followed her all the way back to her cavelike room. In the doorway of the pawnshop next door hung a man's long gown, the bullet hole in its back carefully mended.

Chris was just getting his bearings, trying to figure out where this brothel was, when he foundered.

A dark crowd was swarming outside, coolies from the railroad camps and gold mines. They were rougher than the Chinese men who lived in the city, their queues a little shorter. They had just come out of the only bathhouse in Chinatown, and their faces were taut and shiny.

They were chatting and laughing, hawking and spitting across the alley. Their baggy clothes were covered with creases.

The yard too was packed with men, the shaven part of their skulls striking in the twilight. Cigarette and sundries vendors wandered the crowd. Some of the men sat on the ground, leaning against a wall, their faces numb with expectation.

When Chris walked up, they made way for him. They fell all over themselves to get out of his way.

Two doormen were collecting money in brass basins. Those who paid got a wooden chit to go upstairs. The doormen bellowed like sluice gates too small to stem the surging tide.

A doorman held out his basin to Chris.

He shuddered. He wasn't here to take part in such evil; he was here to wipe it out. The shaven scalps of these men appalled him. They would break her apart; they were instruments of her torture.

When Chris jerked his head up from the basin he saw on the doorman's face an understanding that included him in the uncouth ranks of the other men. He let Chris know it didn't matter if he didn't have the money; he could sample now and tell all his friends.

And then he stuffed a wooden chit into Chris's hand.

He didn't see the loathing in Chris's eyes. He didn't know that this fourteen-year-old white devil was wishing he could set fire to the place so he could charge through the burning evil to rescue the beautiful slave girl on her dying breath. The doorman patted Chris on the shoulder, told him to be patient, told him all Chinese girls were a treat.

The chit in Chris's hand grew damp.

Beneath the lantern light in the doorway, he made out the name scorched into the wood, the same complicated strokes brushed on the door of the room he had visited so often two years before: Fusang.

As night fell, Chris was still walking back and forth outside the two-story building, trying to decide what to do. He finally found the right window. Better have a look first.

The only way up was a small tree. He put one foot on the trunk, braced the other against the building, and started climbing. The tree grew flimsier the closer he got to the top and bowed away with every step he took. He failed many times.

He wasn't sure what he was going to do. He needed to find out if she was in danger. He could still hear the footsteps thundering up and down the wooden stairs.

All his childhood abilities came back to him. With both legs wrapped around the trunk, he kept climbing, the tree swaying like a snake but holding his weight. When he reached the window ledge, he swung back and then flung himself forward, landing on both feet.

The sound made her turn her face toward the window. Her head was nearly buried in her wheat chaff pillow.

By the time he found her eyes, they were already waiting for him. She was no more surprised than if a dove had perched on her window ledge.

Her body was taking in a man. It was sleek with a faint film of sweat. She wasn't resisting as he had expected, but accommodating herself completely to the man. The way the beach accommodates the tide.

CHRIS HAD NEVER IMAGINED IT would be like this.

He thought there should be struggle, some sign of suffering. But what he saw instead was harmony. No matter that the man wore a queue, or that his sallow back was covered with grotesque tattoos—the harmony was beautiful.

Her body was its basis; she controlled the advance and retreat.

The beauty of it set tears coursing down Chris's cheeks.

She watched him without blinking at all, her eyes open wide.

His eyes swelled with tears again, because he saw pleasure in hers. It was the basest kind, the kind that least involves the spirit.

And it did not reside solely in her; the movements of her body spread it to the man, and her gaze sent it toward Chris.

Chris realized that now he was crying for a different reason. With the onslaught of the mysterious pleasure, his body unfolded and quickened in ways he'd never known. The movements of their bodies drew him into their rhythm.

He choked and sobbed, his tears fast and furious, breaking at last into soundless wails.

Her eyes were still wide open, her pink lips arrested as if in the midst of eating. She was watching him, with just a window between them.

Suddenly he thought he understood. Her body was taking in the man, but her eyes and her everything else were taking him in.

Her arms wrapped the tattoo-covered back more tightly, her fingers embedded between the ribs. Her breasts kept shifting shape, and her long black hair, drenched with sweat, streamed from the head of the bed to the floor. The bamboo frame groaned.

Chris's face was bathed in tears now.

The tenth man climbed off her, his eyes like a dead bird's, the last vestiges of his soul seeping through translucent eyelids.

She got up too, and draped a dirty red satin robe over her shoulders. She saw the man to the door, and then walked over behind the curtain. It did nothing to block Chris's view. She no longer looked at him, as if she couldn't see him at all, as if she couldn't see anything. She had spent herself completely; her body didn't count now.

Undismayed by his cry of alarm, she slowly splashed herself with water from the basin to wash off the blood. Her eyes were partly closed as she savored the water splashing on her skin. When she stood up, blood trickled down her legs.

Chris knew about menstruation, but he was still shocked by her attitude toward blood. He had never known anyone to treat it with such nonchalance.

TURN YOUR HEAD JUST A BIT MORE, toward me, no, toward him. That's it; now he can see your face quite clearly through the window. Your concentration as you look at him could bore through all one hundred and sixty of these books caked shut with dust.

As you look at each other, you open yourself to him with your eyes. You invite him in. You watch him enter. You usher him in. You take this outrageously young lover into your body, just via another route.

See? The young white man named Chris is feeling it.

As you watch him, you convince him that suffering is part of your beauty, that you can rise from it again and again, cheeks flushed, whole and full. You, however, are thoroughly unconscious of everything you do.

At this moment you are so utterly beautiful that even I of the same sex stare wide-eyed, like a villager in the big city.

Your suffering moved him. You were responsible for the aberrant standards of love and romance he set at fourteen.

But how could he know he was in love? Or maybe I'm wrong, and he knew exactly what he was going through. To tell you the truth, I'm often wrong about white people. Never mind the white kids of your day. Even with the white man I married I end up in ridiculous conversations because I assume I know what he's thinking.

One time, for instance, I said, This Japanese tofu's terrible, don't buy it again.

He said (not terribly happy, but thoroughly polite), I'm sorry I didn't get what you wanted.

I'm just criticizing the tofu; I'm not blaming you.

I said I was sorry.

I wasn't blaming you; it's the tofu.

Didn't I say I was sorry?

I don't know which of us was more mistaken. So if you think about it, you know just how wrong I can be about Chris. Just as my husband has never been able to hear the unqualified "no" in my "yes."

You let the blood flow. Let him cry out in alarm. This

blood is worth nothing, you seemed to be telling him, just as you are worth nothing. But he would come to find value in worthless things.

You sensed him leave the window. You sensed him climbing the stairs. You sensed him reach your door. But you did not sense the intensity of his feelings. When he pushed open the door, you were sucking on a cold fried river snail. You had just touched up your lips and now they were coated with grease as you spit out an empty shell. He asked if he could come in. You said yes. He had no idea where to begin, as he watched you spit out one snail shell after another. Drops of blood on the floor reflected the candlelight. You finally asked him, How old are you, sir? He looked away. You smiled tenderly, as if to play down this shortcoming. You lifted the kettle from the brazier and blew gently on the cup of tea you poured. Holding his breath, he watched you. You finally bent your head and pecked the surface of the tea—not too hot, just right, you told him with your eyes. Have a seat, you said. You covered and exposed your bare legs with the same insouciance. Your movements were nothing like the gyrations of other prostitutes. Your smile was wholly unguarded.

He blushed. He was thinking about that pleasure. Or he was thinking about the jealousy and disgust he'd felt. I don't know why he blushed. I told you I don't understand whites. Maybe he blushed because he realized what was about to happen, or maybe he choked on the word *love.* His mouth is moving now; let's listen to what he is managing to say.

I've got ten bucks. I can buy you for the night.

Neither of us imagined he would say that. We both stare at him in shock.

He said again, I want to buy you for the night.

This time he spoke slowly and clearly, his voice solid. He showed no trace of the masculine instinct for conquest, just the instant imperiousness of a child. He was intoxicated with his own chivalry. You were bleeding; you'd taken enough for one night.

Your back was to the candlelight at that point, your expression obscure as a statue's—even I fail to read your reaction. No doubt you know how infatuated he is with you. How could you fail to be moved? You reached out to him.

Your fingers traced his cheek, found and fondled his earlobes. Finally I see the expression on your face, but I can't describe it.

You said, If you've got the money, you can come any time.

THE CHINESE COOLIES, who normally started work earlier than anyone else, were nowhere to be seen at the Central Pacific Railroad Company work site. The short men with queues were called yellow worker ants by their white coworkers. They burrowed out from their wooden shacks or earthen shanties before daybreak and filed silently along the mountain ridge, each one barefoot, each one carrying over his shoulder a tin can strung through two punched holes and packed with rice and preserved duck eggs.

They always joined up on the road, and then trudged in silence to the job site a mile away. Because their white coworkers detested their queues, their tin cans packed with rice, their protruding cheekbones, and everything else about them, all the coolies could do was move farther away, out of sight.

It was said that even before full daylight those mud yellow backs were out in full force. But today, the sun now high, there wasn't a single queue in sight.

The foremen believed it at last: The coolies had gone on their first strike.

A supervisor charged all around on horseback without turning up a single poster, slogan, handbill, or any trace of disturbance whatsoever. He looked around helplessly and panicked at the silence.

Two days before, white workers had surrounded a Chinese cook shouldering buckets of tea on his pole. When they left, the old cook was lying face down on the ground, his graying queue lopped off. Beside him lay a piece of paper, on which was written: *This old rat looks almost like a man! Watch out: The boss keeps whole chain gangs of Asiatic rats because they're cheaper!*

Before that, the white workers had threatened a mass strike if hours were not reduced.

The head office had responded, Fine! We'll get coolies to replace you—they work themselves to death and they're cheaper anyway. We can get two of them for the price of one of you.

The emergency recruiting office was swamped for days with men with sallow faces and queues.

What jobs can you do?

Nod energetically.

Oh, you can do anything? We'll give you. . .eighty cents an hour, see you first thing tomorrow on the job.

Nod energetically.

Do you agree to accept full responsibility for all casualties?

Nod energetically.

Okay, put your thumbprint here.

The short men in queues walked out of the recruiting office, their eyes fixed upon the red ink on their thumbs. The white workers watched their delighted faces impassively from the distance.

Once, when laying track through a mountain crevice, thirteen coolies were buried in a landslide. The white workers came running, so grief stricken they temporarily buried their hatred and envy. You must stand with us, brothers, this is slave labor! You're hardly getting paid at all!

Nod energetically.

Stand up! Slavery's been abolished! It's a national crime!

Nod energetically.

Stop letting these slave masters take advantage of you!

Nodding energetically, they picked up their pickaxes and spades and lunch pails.

What are you doing?

Going to work, the men with queues replied.

The white workers finally got it: These Chinese men were the root of all evil, these things that offered themselves up for exploitation. Their equable forbearance made inhuman living conditions, and wages so low they trammeled all human dignity, seem reasonable. Such creatures actually existed, living off a little can of rice and a pinch of salt.

These men in queues collapsed all distance between man and beast and sent the value of man plummeting. These natural born slaves brought masters back from the grave.

The white workers finally understood the whole thing.

Over hundreds of miles of railroad construction, mutterings against coolies grew louder. The fragile peace began to disintegrate.

The coolies began muttering themselves. They talked of giving up and running away, but in the end would clap one another's shoulders and say, Just put up with it. With sad smiles, they would trudge to the job site before the sun broke over the sea, day after day, the same as always.

Only when the old cook fell behind the rest did they realize the necessity of sticking together. By that time, he was already surrounded by thirty-some whites, his graying queue clutched in someone's hand.

The old coolie turned his head, smiling sadly.

That smile, which every coolie knew how to make, enraged the whites, who had originally just meant to toy with him.

He's too old to change his slave ways, they said. The clubs came pounding.

The old coolie's face was covered with blood. Don't kill me! My wife's waiting for me to come home and take care of the ox and the grandchildren, he said to them in broken English.

You old mole, stealing our money to send home to your vermin family!

Don't kill me! I've got an eighty-year-old mother too!

Break his legs and see if he can haul a hundred loads of rock; break his arms and see if he can lay a mile of track; break his teeth in and see if he can live for three days on a single meal!

The old coolie grew smaller and weaker, one leg flapping behind him like an empty sack.

Okay, okay, don't kill me. It's against the law to send my body back. I can't go home to my wife as a can of ashes. Okay, take it easy, you've beaten me pretty good now, save your strength....By this point, he couldn't see anything but blood.

In the time it takes to smoke a cigarette, the whites were walking away, their tension spent.

Unable to rise from the pool of his own blood, the old coolie barely found the strength to call out, Hey, don't go, you can't beat a guy to this stage and then just leave! Okay, okay, give a guy a hand here, put me out of my misery. Come on, it won't take much.

The whites couldn't hear him. A few of them with daggers in their belts surely hadn't heard him, or they would have been all too willing to help out.

Was he dead?

No. He was lying there on his belly trying to find his teeth.

The whites, far away now, were sure he wouldn't die: He could withstand everything else, so he could certainly withstand not dying.

And then a heavy snow fell.

By early morning it had stopped. A man rode up to the old coolie's body and turned it over. He wore a thick black queue and huge rings on all four fingers of his right hand. Two women rode behind in a wagon, their faces powdered, penciled, and painted identically.

Ah Ding was back. As always, each time he disappeared into the sea he changed his name; this time he was called Da Yong. He believed that by changing his name he could add someone else's power and intelligence to his own.

Da Yong held the stiff corpse in his arms and looked at him. He decided his old face was too ugly, so he smoothed back the gray hair. But it didn't help. He whipped out a white handkerchief and tried to wipe the blood off the coolie's face, but couldn't. So he just covered it with the handkerchief. As a rule, Da Yong never left the people he killed looking this bad. He wasn't satisfied until he had wiped off all the blood, straightened the hair, and removed any expression of terror or incomprehension from the face. Then he straightened his (or her) collar, and adjusted the pants. Death was one's final appearance on stage, so one could hardly go out looking bad. It was simply inexcusable. The dead would not tolerate it, and Da Yong wouldn't either. Da Yong just couldn't stand seeing the old fellow looking so bad in death, so meek and miserable, and beaten to a pulp besides.

He carried him to the wagon and told the women to get down.

He picked up the notice about Asiatic rats.

After they'd gone some distance, Da Yong looked back to see the whores straggling along behind with the pigeon-toed gait of women with bound feet, the purple of their frozen faces showing through their makeup. He would sell them in the next town; they were worth a fortune in the small towns around here.

They started up a mountain. Looking down, Da Yong saw the black heads of the coolies all over the valley. The coolies had to cross this mountain to get to the job site.

A smattering of snowflakes brushed Da Yong's face. He pursed his fleshy lips, his gaze distant beneath the low dark clouds of his eyelids. Nowadays, whenever a scheme was about to occur to him, his face took on this expression, pensive, yet completely vacant, laced with despair.

When those who knew him well saw this face, they would begin to doubt he was the same person; maybe the name changes really did give him a new personality.

Changing names gave him a pleasure like that of reincarnation. You could shirk all the debts accrued in your previous life, under your former name. At times, even he would forget his own past, who he really was.

A POSTMAN ROWED DOWN to a village by the water twice a month.

The women lined up on the bank to receive the money sent home by their husbands, sons, or brothers overseas.

Sometimes the postman would say, Nothing for you, no letter for Ah Ji!

She would chase his boat as if it were her own soul. Nothing? Nothing for me?

He wouldn't have the heart to keep teasing her. He'd burst out laughing and hand her an envelope of money.

She would spit a lichee pit in his face, but because she was faint with panic, the pit would travel only a few inches before falling to the ground.

There were hardly any men in the village. The men were those envelopes that came across the ocean each month.

There weren't any thatched houses in the village either. The money in those envelopes became sturdy black roof tiles that sheltered the women from wind and rain.

Every eight or ten years, when he had earned enough for his passage, a man would come home, and when he left again a woman would be pregnant. When he went ashore at Gold Mountain he would draw a blank line in the space below his name, for the name of the son in the womb. If the baby was a girl, that blank could be sold, not for some outrageous price but just enough for another ticket, so he could go home and try again.

One day another group of men left the village. That night, a family was out searching the place for their eight-year-old Ah Tai. Someone said he'd seen him go off with the men who were going overseas.

When Ah Tai was fifteen, he made off with two horses from a gold mine. When he arrived in Gold Mountain City, he was a tall, handsome youth named Ah Kui.

Ah Kui worked at a cigar factory by day, and frequented whorehouses and gambling dens at night. If he owed someone money, he'd challenge him to fight for it; if someone owed him, he'd get his money back and then beat him within an inch of his life anyway.

By the time he was seventeen, he no longer had to work for wages at all, for along with selling nude photos of himself in the brothels, he had begun breaking in horses. With the horses he stole, he'd been studying the nature of the beast. He discovered you couldn't tame a horse with strength alone, for man would always be weaker than the horse. Instead, you had to use torture. He could bring a horse under control in two or three days, using shapes, colors, and sounds to terrorize it, and then hunger, thirst, and the whip. The horses he tamed were always just a step away from madness. This made them the best runners, and the most submissive.

After a while, he landed a job at the racetrack. He was twenty, and had already killed five people and nine horses.

He'd finagled the racetrack job with a five-hundred-dollar bribe. By then he'd spent years studying the wins and losses of every horse.

He struck up an acquaintance with two whites, one a bank teller, the other a stockbroker. By spending lavishly, he quickly cultivated their friendship. He'd known for a long time that they had both lost so much at the races that their wives had left them. One day he said to them, I can guarantee you a winner, but you'll have to give me half.

Since they didn't have anything to lose, they said, Okay, we'll give you sixty percent.

Just do what I say. Bet on the horse I tell you. I'll stake you.

Okay, whatever horse you say.

When you win, you give me my share immediately.

Okay, half, right?

Sixty percent, you just said.

Okay. You fucking Chinaman.

When you win, keep your damned mouths shut. You can't tell anyone I'm behind this.

If we lose? Jesus.

You won't. If you lose you can shoot me. Nothing ever

happens when you white devils kill a Chinaman anyway.

You don't look like you'd be all that easy to kill.

Don't worry, it won't come to that. But when you win, don't even think of running off with the money. I'd kill you sooner than a raccoon.

Staring at this Chinaman, the white devils realized for the first time that a man with a queue could be dauntless, even dangerous.

He staked them each three hundred dollars for horse number 5, and then made himself scarce.

They regretted this bet immediately. The very first lap out, number 5 fell behind almost all the other horses. It was nearly a half lap behind the front runner number 8.

They wished they'd skimmed a little off the top of their stakes for a stiff drink. When number 5 was passed by yet another horse, they wished they'd just run off with the money. With three hundred bucks you could move far away and remarry.

But on the fourth lap, number 5 passed two horses.

In the fifth lap, it passed three.

By the eighth lap, it finally passed number 9, the mighty champion.

The two men jumped out of their seats.

Number 5 was leading all comers. Number 5 was leading by two laps. Number 5 won. In the blink of an eye, three hundred dollars had become a fortune. The two of them leaned on each other to keep from falling over.

When they arrived at the beach where they were to

meet, he was waiting, naked, flexing his muscles, the tip of his queue clamped between his teeth. His five daggers were freshly sharpened, and he was in the process of smearing something on the tips. The two eyed each other: the poison, no doubt.

He had lit a bonfire nearby, and they smelled something cooking in the tin can hanging over it.

He walked over, took the money from them, and said, Have some lunch while I count this. He pointed to the can.

What is it?

Fur coat. Eat it and you won't have to spend a dime on coats in the cold.

Tastes great, looks terrible, the teller said.

The texture of this meat is quite. . .interesting, the broker added.

Have as much as you like, make yourselves at home. He grinned, his big white teeth showing between his fleshy lips.

You Chinamen eat everything but flies.

Says who? We eat flies.

You'll eat anything, a pig from head to tail, a dog from front door to back. There's probably only one part you don't eat. They winked at each other. Just that one part . . .

That's white-devil slander.

Who were they to deny it? They ate with gusto, their faces covered with grease, their hats pushed to the back of their heads. You people even eat blood, the small gut, the large gut, anything! Their voices took on an accusing tone.

He slowly stuck the daggers one by one back into his belt. Hey, that stuff's for losers. Get this: We can pass up any food you name, just throw it out. There's only one thing we just can't pass up.

They abruptly stopped chewing, as if stricken with a toothache, and looked into their bowls.

You can't tell what you're eating? Dick.

They froze, their mouths bulging with purple meat.

As a rule, your four-leggeds make better eating than your two-leggeds. He showed his big teeth again when he smiled.

The two men bolted to the rocks and vomited.

They were so pathetic, he thought, puking so hard they were jerking, their necks distended beyond the width of their heads, as if they would turn themselves inside out like socks. When they came back, the skin on their necks looked like freshly plucked gooseflesh.

He waited.

They reached into their breast pockets and gave him the rest of what he had coming.

After the second and third wins, the bank teller announced he was quitting, as he handed over the spoils. He said he'd made more than he'd ever dreamed and didn't want to get greedy.

The fourth time, the broker realized he'd picked up a

tail, a man in a wide-brimmed Stetson. He wanted to quit but couldn't bring himself to do it.

He said, I'm sure that PI has a line on me.

Just one? At least three, the Chinaman said, slowly chewing his plug.

If they arrest me, I'm bound to talk the first time they hit me!

Nothing to be ashamed of, it's human nature. Who wants men to be as loyal as dogs? If it were me, I'd confess *before* taking a beating. You spare yourself and you spare them too.

The police found the stockbroker dead on a street corner a few days later.

They cracked the case with the help of the private detective. The Chinaman who had made such a name for himself with horses was behind the whole thing. He'd mixed an herbal sedative into the feed of all the horses, all but one, that is. The sedative worked as a muscle relaxant, inducing an undetectable lethargy. Naturally the only horse that hadn't been drugged came in first.

For months on end, the detectives hunted the Chinese horse tamer named Ah Kui.

But he didn't return to Chinatown for three years, until the case had grown completely cold. He ignored anyone who called him Ah Kui. He had a clean slate of a name: Ah Ding. The police department had gone through three chiefs in three years. One had been thrown out of office for bribery, one fired for incompetence. The third either had forgotten or simply didn't want to bother with the racetrack scam.

And so the free spirit Ah Ding appeared in Chinatown. He dressed in the most expensive clothes, wore a British hat, and carried a leather jewelry case around with him. This case held his everyday jewelry. When in a good mood, he might wear three different pocket watches in a single day. The case also doubled as a wallet; he was known to stake his jewelry when luck was with him at the gambling tables.

When he was satisfied with the service he got at a brothel—that is, when his chin drooped over the edge of the bed and he was too sapped even to chew tobacco—he would rummage around in his jewelry case for a bracelet or choker to give the girl.

Then he'd call out with a deep sigh, Ah Tao!. . .No? Ah Xiu!. . .wrong again? Ah Ping! . . .

The girl would apologetically tell him he'd gotten her name wrong.

He would roll his eyes and sigh more deeply, What's the difference? Be a good girl for me now and get the hell out of here.

Then he'd lie there on his stomach, still as death, watching the blue incense smoke trapped in the room.

No one knew where he really lived. And no one knew he had a weakness: his longing for the wife he'd never even seen.

This was the wife his parents had married in for him,

said to be kind and virtuous. He imagined what she looked like: her face, her hands, the beautiful curve of her back when she pushed the millstone, the slight jiggle of her breasts when she trotted down the mountain with a load of kindling on her back (much better than the naked but shopworn breasts around here), her profile at sewing or embroidery when she lowered and tilted her head to bite off a thread. Sometimes, not very often, he would even imagine what she was like making love. It nearly drove him crazy. She was passionate and contained at the same time, gazing at him with such sincerity in her eyes, the delicate hairs on her upper lip beaded with tiny drops of sweat. . . .

He didn't know why he longed for her so. He was like a drifter forced to take to the road, or a weary seasoned traveler who has stayed in too many inns and eaten too many fancy meals, who yearned for home, a place to go back to, no matter how vague or far away, no more than a distant mirage on the highway.

Ah Ding believed only one person could make him nice and ordinary, and that was his wife. The day she appeared, he would roll on the ground and slough the hide from his body, like someone under a sorcerer's spell who finally turns back into himself after having been all sorts of things.

When Ah Ding resurfaced he was already Da Yong. During the gold rush, when everyone was coming and going—when everyone was making history, pioneering the present, cutting off the future—he had another clean slate.

COMING DOWN THE MOUNTAIN, Da Yong ran into the coolies on their way up. They made way for him, the wagon, and the two whores following ten paces behind. In the light reflecting off the snow, the coolies' faces were haggard, the color of bile. They swept their eyes over the perfumed women and looked away. For all their sweet finery, those beauties couldn't possibly soothe their aches and pains.

Da Yong reined in his horse and looked down at the men flanking his path. Veiled disdain gave way to a nasty smirk. He jumped off his horse and yanked the tarp off the wagon to uncover the old coolie. The frozen blood had begun to thaw and the wind ruffled the gray hair, no longer held in place by the queue, no longer sticky with blood. The old coolie seemed to stir.

The men couldn't decide whether or not to go on to work.

Someone finally recognized the corpse, and gasped, It's the old cook! He was bringing us tea yesterday and took a shortcut.

Take a good long look. See how his hair's been lopped off? How his skull's bashed in? Take a good long look, Da Yong cried out like a street vendor.

Someone walked up to the corpse's head and said, Holy shit, all his teeth got knocked out!

Yep, Da Yong said, eating just won't be the same for the old man.

At this point a few men at the edge of the crowd slowly broke away. Da Yong asked, Where are you going?

To work, we'll be late.

Da Yong looked at them with a smile, looked at them for a good long time.

As if they had nowhere to put their faces, they shifted their eyes right and left under his gaze.

Da Yong said, These two whores here, my treat. Everybody gets a turn. See you in town.

He took the corpse out of the wagon, lifted the whores back in, and went on his way.

From that day on, coolies were nowhere to be seen on the job.

No one knew that the mastermind behind the strike was Da Yong—eating, drinking, whoring, and gambling in town.

All five thousand coolies stopped work.

Da Yong dashed by their shacks on horseback, drunkenly tossing pamphlets at each door.

This strike announcement, who wrote it?

Read it to me, Da Yong said, feigning both slurred speech and illiteracy.

Do you know how long this strike's supposed to last?

What's a strike? Da Yong asked with earnest ignorance.

The coolies' strike made big news in the papers. Railroad stocks plummeted in a single morning. By their silent and thorough disappearance, the coolies had made their existence known.

In the seventh hour of the strike, the owners sent someone to tell them that new recruitment had already begun. If they wouldn't work, the railroad could always get cheaper Chinese who would.

The coolies lowered their heads, and their eyes began to shift back and forth.

If you come back to work in the next hour, we'll pay you twice your original wages. An hour later and you'll only get one and a half times what you used to. After three o'clock this afternoon, you'll only get a dime more. If you try to come back tomorrow, sorry, you're too late, because we start striking names off the rolls tonight.

Two coolies followed the man back to work.

An hour later, fifty more coolies had rushed to the job site. The first two strike breakers, seeing what an example they'd become, laughed and shouted, Hell, we've got everything against whites, but nothing against their money!

The fifty men stood impassively ten paces away. One of them said, Looks like we have traitors after all.

Another said, Break their legs.

The two froze, thinking they'd heard wrong.

Strike headquarters has decided to break your legs. Two traitors, four dog's legs.

The two were caught and each tied to a tree trunk.

Don't break our legs, they pleaded, we've still got to squat to shit!

Okay, we'll beat your faces in. We'll break your noses!

Break our legs, then, anything but our faces!

A thousand more men came running. Originally they'd been swayed by the owners' representative to break the strike, but when they saw the traitors tied up there, losing every last scrap of face of eight generations of ancestors, they joined in, shouting, Traitors! Break their legs!

What should I hit first? A man holding a big stick and taking measure of the four legs solicited opinions from the crowd.

The little leg in the middle, someone intoned.

When the traitors heard this, they cried out, Brothers, have a heart; we've got nothing here in this devil country, no paddies, no fields, no wife, no opera. Whoring's the only fun we've got, and only once a month at that; if you hit us there, we won't have any fun at all!

You think you can still go whoring? Do the brothels want traitors? the man with the stick asked the crowd.

No! Not even old sows want traitors.

As the stick landed, gleeful shouting drowned out the cries of pain.

From a distance, all one could see was the quivering leaves of the two trees.

Da Yong watched from afar, his hands tucked into the opposite sleeves of his mink coat.

Coolies filled mountain and plain. The snow was churned like a freshly plowed field. The birds clattered into one another, scared out of their wits by the sudden appearance of so many men in queues.

Two owners' representatives looked on, open mouthed.

They asked Da Yong, You're not with them?

I'm not with anybody, Da Yong replied.

They noticed that Da Yong had chosen a good spot— one outcropping of rock fronted by another, offering a perfect view and perfect cover at the same time. They said to him, Hey, come down from there.

You want me to come down?

That's right. And then go stand over there.

Why?

We want that spot.

This spot here? It'll cost you two bucks. Four for the both of you.

They were surprised at first, then quickly smiled with distaste.

Da Yong held out his hand, rings on all fingers, waiting for the money to land in his palm.

Damn, I thought only Jews were capable of that kind of move.

Don't give Jews all the credit, Da Yong said as he began counting the coins in his hand.

What're they shouting? Translate for us.

That's a separate transaction. What'll you pay?

Christ. Here's a buck.

They said, Those white devil sons of bitch whores just passed a new law. They're going to deport all Chinese. They said, Those big-nosed sons of bitch whores white devils, with their smelly armpits and ape fur . . .

You don't have to translate the details.

You get all that for a buck—I've got to give you your money's worth. They're saying, the new law makes the Chinese the only immigrants to be deported; this is outright racial oppression. And they're saying, the railroad bosses attribute the completion of the railroad to the rigor of the Germans, the endurance of the British, and the happy-go-lucky spirit of the Irish, without a single mention of Chinese coolies, whom they've always worked like mules.

The representatives nodded gravely. Go on.

They're saying, Each day of injustice is another strike day. . . .

Why are you stopping? This is the most critical part. . . .

That's all you get for a buck.

They stared at this Chinese fellow, resplendent in his garb and jewels. And what they saw was a face more honest than a dog's.

DA YONG POCKETED THE MONEY, mounted his horse, and rode off.

By the time the strike had all four shareholders turning to stiff drink, he was already on his way to Gold Mountain City.

DON'T MOVE, Fusang. Let me have a look at your drained face.

As I said when we first met, you're old. Even before you became famous, you were too old. Most girls did not live so long. First their wishes and dreams and fantasies died, one after another; and then all the men who vowed to brave oceans and mountains for them, to take them away to be wives and mothers, died in their hearts, one after the next. The last thing to die was their bodies, the one death that wasn't painful.

You turn your face to the window. A strand of the bead curtain breaks and beads fall like tears. The thick wooden bars break the light into stripes, and in this light I clearly see the shadows of illness on your face. The flush of your fever has faded, and now you have the same sallow complexion and aged eyes of all the girls who ended up where you're about to.

They call it a hospital.

You see the plans I have for describing it and smile with terror.

No one comes back to see you. Your johns forget you the minute they walk out your door.

Chris doesn't come either. I know he's the real reason your face is turned toward the window. Ten days ago, he was right outside it, his face bathed in tears.

You should know, his love for you is what made me decide to write your story. People just don't love like that anymore. Love these days entails so many other considerations: green cards, jobs, white collar versus blue collar, Honda versus BMW; when the subject of love comes up, we grimace behind each other's back.

I scoured those one hundred and sixty histories of San Francisco with a vengeance in search of clues to the feelings between you and Chris. The clues were faint indeed. Sometimes you became someone else entirely, and he was either made to sound typical or singled out for condemnation. I figure the reason he sounded so typical was this: So many white boys visited Chinese prostitutes that the historians just kept reproducing one another's accounts, errors and all, until Chris became just one more john between the ages of eight and fourteen, buried in the statistics. Boy johns were a social phenomenon, particularly white boy johns of Chinese prostitutes, and when these two particular circumstances combined, Chris's own particularity got lost. Maybe, as the historians saw it, he really wasn't unique. It's impossible to say that Chris was the only one of the thousands of boys who had genuine feelings for a Chinese prostitute. Maybe they all did. Everybody knows that boys seldom remain unmoved by their first woman. At the very least, the experience becomes a secret memory that lasts their whole lives. It's simply that no one has bothered to understand these boys case by case. As soon as they become a social phenomenon, they can only exist in generalization.

You hear the usual comings and goings in the hall, the coquettish bickering. Where is that boy? You keep looking at me, knowing that I am the only one who knows.

In the waning light after sunset everything in your room grows bleak.

You wait calmly for someone to bring you a drink of water, but no one does. But you don't mind. Your calm has nothing to do with the word *endurance,* the character I see on scrolls in nearly every Chinese home, mounted so carefully and hung so conspicuously, with its connotations of gritted teeth, the mouth saying yes while the heart says no. I've never had the guts to ask what this word really means. Once, when I saw it in the living room of a forty-year-old Chinese student, I stood there for a long time, afraid that if I turned away too quickly its owner would notice the cynicism in my eyes. I figured that since the word was calligraphed with such emphasis and affectation, I had to be missing something.

Just the way you take in each customer, you calmly take in death as it climbs onto you and enters your body. You hear it creaking the bamboo bed. You feel it shyly touching your lips, your chest, your nipples.

Do you hear the footsteps on the stairs? It's those men with the rope stretcher, coming to take the dying to the hospital. You hear the scratchy fiddle creak of a few doors opening, then closing, and the voice of a woman saying, The soul snatchers are back again.

MORNING COMES TO THE BROTHEL at lunchtime. Two or three doors open and men come out, their pants hastily tied at the waists, their heels crushing the backs of their shoes, the hair falling out of their queues. They are the johns who stayed the night. They look away when they pass in the hall or on the stairs. If they can't avoid meeting head on, they exchange cigarettes and winks and a few words only the other understands.

After Ah Mian saw her john off, she went down the hall carrying her baby, knocking at doors. Everyone ignored her—with the customers gone, they were all catching up on their sleep.

Finding Fusang's door unlatched, she pushed it open and went in.

Fusang shifted to the far side of the bed so Ah Mian could lay the baby down. Ah Mian was fifteen.

I didn't hear him crying last night.

He's a good boy; I put him under the bed.

You weren't afraid the rats would get him?

I broke a cracker into four pieces, put them around him, and when I checked on him this morning, the crackers were gone and the baby was fine.

Ah Mian unwrapped the swaddling and whipped off the blanket, and the two-month-old baby rolled out, face down, his whole butt blue.

My little baby's leaving today, she said, Third Uncle's taking him. To sell him, far away.

Is Third Uncle his father? Fusang asked.

Is Third Uncle this pretty? Ah Mian replied. If he's sold off, the son goddess won't give me another. Ah Mian had aborted four pregnancies. The last fetus had held on, though, even when the drugs hurled Ah Mian off the bed to the floor. When the baby was finally born, those at the bedside secretly counted its limbs and features. Much to their surprise, everything was intact.

Just as Ah Mian was about to speak again, Fusang started coughing. She had been running a fever for a week now, and her customers had dropped off by half. She coughed so hard at night that the johns in adjacent rooms were complaining.

Ah Mian said, Stop coughing, I've got a favor to ask you.

Fusang kept coughing.

Fusang, I want to ask you to be the baby's father.

Fusang was panting and choking and staring at her through watery eyes. This was not an unusual request. Men spoke of marriage all the time, but once the promise escaped their lips, they disappeared. When a woman realized she was waiting in vain, she and a friend would secretly make quick vows to heaven and earth. If they got sick or ran into trouble, someone was duty-bound to take care of them. They had a confidante when they needed to discuss something private or bitch; they had someone to wash their backs and scratch their mosquito bites for them.

Fusang agreed to be the baby's father. Ah Mian had

come to her only because no one else had answered the door.

Ah Mian said, Hold him down for me while I tie this mole off.

Okay.

This is an unlucky spot for a mole; it means he'd be carrying kindling, pond mud, and debt on his back his whole life.

Uh hunh.

Just like this mole of mine. Ah Mian pointed to her own back.

She wrapped a thread around the grayish growth on the baby's back, yanked it tight, and jerked. Blood trickled out. She pressed a pinch of incense ash into the hole.

Fusang's coughing was drowned out by the baby's wailing.

Ah Mian said, You keep coughing like that and you're going to put a big hole in your chest.

Fusang managed to nod between the violent spasms.

Ah Mian continued, My dad had a hole there big as the eye of an ox; my mom sold me to pay for stopping it up.

Fusang could no longer continue this conversation, for she was coughing herself to pieces.

When Third Uncle came to take the baby away that night, all the women in the building came out to see them off. They slapped Third Uncle on the head and arms and back, saying things like, So you're back with more of your cheating and killing, Third Uncle?

Long time no see, Third Uncle, what've you been up to? Your usual deficiencies of character?

Hey Third Uncle, what's that meat in your basket? How're you gonna cook it?

When the foreigners set that fire the other day, we said spare us all, but burn Third Uncle's house right down to the ground!

Don't even leave him the ashes! Bake him to a crisp! Or cook him down into one big greasy longevity tonic!

Third Uncle was cackling like a goose, his head bobbing on his lengthening and shortening neck. To keep him from leaving, the girls were grabbing his collar, the crotch of his pants, or his rat's tail of a queue—the little hair he had left.

He backed his way to the staircase squealing, You little bitches! Is this any way to treat your third uncle?

One of the girls said, Hey, stay a while and we'll cook you up a nice big pot of dicks. Strengthen your manhood! You can put it in, but it falls right out with one little cough!

The baby in the basket was crying his head off. When Third Uncle left, the girls were still laughing so hard they had to hold one another up. Ah Mian was laughing the hardest and babbling over the fact that she had forgotten the tiger booties she'd made for her baby. She melted to the floor with laughter.

Ah Mian was laughing so hard even Fusang crawled out of bed to lean in the doorway.

When everyone stopped laughing, they picked the

puddle of Ah Mian up off the floor, clucking and scolding her to stop laughing; she was driving everybody crazy.

Ah Mian never stopped.

When Fusang grew so sick she couldn't even cough anymore, Ah Mian ran off. Her laughter shattered the peace of the whole street. Everyone got out of her way, so shaken they forgot their teeth on the outside of their lips.

No one knew where Ah Mian went. Third Uncle searched for forty-nine days without turning up a single lead. He said to the madam, If only I'd sold off the two of them together!

With Ah Mian gone, one of her dates was foisted off on Fusang, who swallowed a pinch of opium to stop her cough, and with a little extra powder and rouge was more or less presentable.

A commotion in the middle of the night woke everyone in the building. A john dashed out of Fusang's room with her silk robe draped over his shoulders, one hand dragging Fusang, the other holding a bloody towel. He was shouting for someone to go get Amah Mei.

You trying to put this on my head? How do you expect me to explain it if she dies? Her TB at this stage! As he hiked his torso with each indignant shout, his penis escaped the embroidered hem of the garment and swung against his thighs. I want my money back, and if I catch TB from her, you're paying for my medicine too!

Naked but for a camisole, Fusang was held upright by

the hand clutching her hair. Only half awake, she wasn't sure what the guy was yelling about.

He continued, Get a white devil cop in here right now; they're looking all over town for Chinese TB devils.

Everyone tried to persuade him, If you go for the cops there's no need to take Fusang with you.

The john said, Evidence! Otherwise, you'll bury her out back the minute I'm gone and I'll have no proof!

It's not like a cat covering its shit, they said. She won't be that easy to bury.

He shouted, Who's gonna go get the cops? There's a station at the corner!

Fusang was still groggy; if she hadn't been held up by the hair, she would have lain down on the floor from the start.

Someone noticed blood on the floor of her room, glistening like lacquer in the candlelight.

The john was still shouting when another customer came up the stairs and stood there with his arms crossed over his chest. After listening for a moment, he walked up and knocked the angry john in the head with his ring-bedecked fist, sending him crumpling to the floor.

The customer looked at Fusang, then turned to the people in the hall: Go back to bed.

The next morning, the girls all pressed to the window to watch Da Yong leave. They knew all about him: He mainly used his daggers for hunting and fishing. He hardly needed so much weaponry to kill a person. He only resorted to the daggers when he truly had no other option. But once he did, even the white devil police would leave him alone, for what he threw was the decoy double dagger. When his victims saw the dagger in his right hand aiming for the space between their eyebrows, they ducked, only to find themselves the target of the dagger in his left hand. But they never knew which dagger was meant to hit them. No one had ever actually seen this technique, for before it ever came to that, he'd already decided everything with his fists.

Fusang was the only one not pressed against the window watching him go.

After Da Yong left, the girls went back to sleep. Fusang was returned to her bed without even knowing how she got there and drifted in and out of consciousness until two men came for her with a stretcher. They wore black jackets, black pants, and black Stetson hats—in the dark stairway, they were completely invisible.

They deftly cleared the hallway. Those who opened their doors to look quickly shut and bolted them fast.

This was before the customers arrived, when the girls were all bathing, putting on perfume, setting out candles, tuning their *qin* strings.

The men entered Fusang's room.

She awoke when a hand at her nostrils was checking to see if she was dead. When they saw her eyes open, they looked for something to gag her with. One grabbed a towel from the floor, bunched it up, and hid it behind his back with the intention of stuffing it in her mouth by surprise.

Fusang, however, suddenly opened her mouth wide, like a baby swallow awaiting food.

That startled them all right, and there was a moment of awkwardness before the man with the towel tossed it away. For a woman like her, so used to the gag, it was not simply overkill but embarrassing. As if they had sorely underestimated her.

Fusang didn't move or make a sound when they wrapped her in the quilt, wrapped her so tightly not a gap of light was left. Then they put her on the stretcher.

Still no one came to stop the thieves in black. Those who knew they were there were least inclined to come out of their rooms, to avoid another meeting with them later. The men were hired to carry off corpses, though occasionally they would take someone about to become one.

They went down the stairs without a sound.

The staircase was so narrow that anyone on the way up would block it completely.

On his way up was a fourteen-year-old little white devil, his blue eyes fixed on the stretcher. He suddenly clamped his hand over his nose and mouth.

Grinning, their eyes completely shadowed by their hats, the men in black asked him to get out of the way.

He pressed himself to the wall as tightly as he could. The stretcher brushed his belly as it went by.

the end of the stretcher passed him, violent cough-
erupted from the quilt.

The little white devil gasped. He recognized the sound
of that cough. But before he could figure out what was
going on, they had already made it down the stairs and
were headed for the backyard.

The men in black pushed the warped back hatch open.

The little white devil followed them, his pale blue eyes
paling further with his stare.

Wait!

They muttered to each other, Fuck the mother. Quick-
ening their steps, they tried to maneuver the stretcher
through the hatchway but it kept getting stuck.

Stop! Stop, I say!

No understand English.

They finally made it. A buggy was parked at the junc-
tion of the cobblestone alley and road. Weeds were growing between the stones. Cigarette papers on the garbage
heap flapped like wings as if to fly away. The last light of
day sapped all substance from the horse and buggy, turning everything to shadow.

Dusk fog drifted in.

The little white devil chased them out the back hatch.
Stop! Hold it right there!

We no English.

Violent coughing erupted once more from the quilt.
One end of the stretcher was already through the buggy
curtain.

Damn, I knew we should have gagged her.

Knock her out with that stick.

Yeah, and the little white devil makes a perfect eye-witness.

He can't see anything from there. Let's get it over with.

Okay, you do it.

No, you.

The little white devil had no idea what they were being so polite about.

Hold it right there or I'll call the cops!

No English, no English.

For better or worse the stretcher was in the buggy now. One of the men in black went to untether the horse while the other picked up the big stick. If the little white devil called the cops, they could hit him once to knock him out for a few minutes and make their getaway.

But the little white devil turned around and ran back toward the yard.

CHRIS RAN BACK INTO THE YARD, through the building, and to the stable out front to get his horse. But when he circled around back, the buggy was nowhere in sight, and even the clopping was gone.

He sat all alone on his horse. He didn't know where to go.

When it got dark, he returned to the brothel. The lamps upstairs were lit and music could be heard. The little girl who delivered fruit to the rooms passed him in the hall.

Sure enough, Fusang was gone. An old man was

squatting on the floor of her room wiping up the congealed blood. He looked up at Chris without stopping.

Where did she go?

The old man just kept looking at Chris and wiping.

Did she go to the hospital?

The old man slowly pushed the door closed. It lingered a crack before closing completely.

Chris was now on the street. He had forgotten his evening Latin lesson. He forgot all about his curfew.

He searched street by street. The sky turned from dark to light.

THE KOEHLER FAMILY CAME from Germany. Typical northern Germans, anxiety-ridden, tight-lipped.

If someone at the enormous dinner table said, Windy today, wasn't it? everyone would look up in surprise, wondering what had made him so talkative all of a sudden.

If someone said, The Sydney ducks started a fire north of the city, it would take a full five minutes before someone else would say, It must have been terrible.

Another five minutes or so later, The police are rounding up suspects.

After yet another five minutes, No doubt they set the fire to destroy evidence.

Born criminals!

We ought to throw them all back to Australia.

But mostly what got burned down were Chinese houses.

You call those things houses?

After someone finished speaking at that dinner table, the pause that followed would lead any outsider to conclude that the conversation had no chance of continuing. But five minutes later, he would discover that it had never really stopped, it was just continuing in silence. Before a speaker put forth his own words, he had to take in those of the previous speaker, turn them over in his mind, and mentally rehearse his own response (all the while making sure he wasn't about to rob someone else of his turn to speak). The final step was to swallow the food in his mouth.

Because the Koehler family were people of few words, every one of them was a poet. They saw poetry in everything, they just didn't recite it. Or perhaps they just recited it with their eyes. Their eyes were deep but not very responsive, because they had to linger on a thing long enough for the poem to move from the eyes to the brain and then from the brain back to the eyes.

Oddly, not a single one of them ever picked up a pen to write down the poem passing through his head at any given moment. Or perhaps by the time a poem had gone from mind to pen it had become something else entirely. Yet they read a lot of poetry. When they emigrated from Germany, they could only bring one box of books, all poetry except for the Bible.

The Koehlers were military men. All the men in the family had a mistress on the side—American Indian, South American, gypsy, or Mayan women.

Chris's father and uncle had twelve children between them, and they all lived together in a little town south of San Francisco. Chris was the ninth child in the two families, and as a result, neither his eccentricities nor his virtues received a whole lot of attention. The men in the family took a certain military pride in their own austere conduct, so they never noticed how Chris was betraying his heritage. They never noticed the way he would gasp, Oh, no! through clenched teeth at the sight of something beautiful or strange. Or how an Oriental whore he thought beautiful beyond all compare could wrest such feeling from him.

He determined without the slightest hesitation that this was love. Because it entailed such suffering. None of the love in poetry was about happiness—it was all about pain. To a boy of fourteen, pain was much more novel than happiness, and far more romantic.

His obsession with her made him neglect his homework and offend the servants. And on this April evening, it rippled the customary silence at the dinner table.

Where were you the night before last? His father gave Chris the first attentive look he'd received from him in years.

Chris chewed his meat and then leisurely swallowed and dabbed his lips with his snow white napkin. I had a makeup Latin lesson, he said, looking at his father.

Five minutes later, his father said, I see you don't understand English. He switched to German, Where were you the night before last?

Chris remained calm, hoping to come up with an answer before swallowing the food in his mouth. It would be stupid to lie again, for his father held nothing but contempt for those who told the same lie twice. To lie again after one knew he had been found out was sheer idiocy.

Unable to tell the truth, Chris broke off the staring contest with his father.

I had a note from your Latin teacher. His father passed a folded piece of paper to the person sitting next to him.

The note passed from hand to hand like a pepper shaker. In this household, showing any emotion at all was considered tasteless and undignified. When the note reached Chris, his father said, You have my permission to read it.

Pursing his lips, Chris picked up the note, but instead of opening it he carefully put it in his breast pocket. He knew that to read it here would be scandalous. Ignoring the note might make his father mad, but refusing to give up his self-respect would infuriate him.

Instead, his father's expression softened.

By acting the way his father would, Chris had won his forgiveness. But the effort exhausted him and he longed for his mother.

FUSANG'S EYES GRADUALLY PENETRATED the darkness.

The hospital had eight bunk beds. As her eyes focused further, she noticed a shoe under one of the other beds. It lay there like a lone boat grounded in the shallows.

The bed was empty, but Fusang felt sure that the shoe was still warm.

The room smelled of damp plaster. Fresh mildew gave off its own peppery scent. A drop of water fell between her eyebrows.

She opened her eyes so wide they seemed to swell, to keep vigil over her own life. If you let your eyes close now you're done for.

As the men in black were leaving, Fusang had asked, Are you going to lock the door?

They were stunned: She had actually uttered a complete sentence, and her tongue didn't sound swollen at all.

If we don't, you'll run, one of them said, teasing.

Fusang said, Oh. She couldn't tell whether she would run or not.

The other one said, Be a good girl and go to sleep now. Tomorrow the doctor will come and see you.

The men had no interest in chatting all day. They hurriedly loaded the owner of the shoe onto the stretcher and headed out the door.

Fusang asked, Are you going to bury or cremate her?

Bury, cremate, she won't know the difference, one of them said.

Wait until I'm completely dead before you cremate me.

Don't you worry, the doctor will be able to tell.

Just as they were about to close the door, Fusang said, If she was really dead, her shoe would never have fallen off. She wanted to tell them a dead girl's feet would stiffen straight up because they'd know this was the only pair of shoes they'd get. They didn't want to go over to the other side with one foot bare.

But the door had already closed, so she let it go.

Another drop of water fell between her eyebrows. She turned her head to take the next one somewhere else. It would be better to move her whole body, but she didn't have the energy just now. The itch in her throat was gone too. It would have brought on a coughing spell, which would have warmed her up some.

The constant smell of blood was gone as well. That blood smelled so nice—she could smell herself.

This cool comfort was death. Fusang would rather be aching now, for that kept her alive, whereas comfort meant death. She wanted that scorching pain again, like the first time she'd been with a man.

She couldn't remember who he was. All she remembered was the pain. By the time her whole body stiffened and her jaw clenched, she discovered a grain of pleasure. You had to cross all the way through the pain to reach it. If you resisted, your anger would hold you back. As she let herself collide with the pain, sparks ignited, pleasure quickened.

In that moment, she experienced the renewal of a fish just scaled by the knife.

When the man who took her virginity sensed Fusang nearly kicking with pain, he stopped panting and tightened his legs around her as if reining in a horse. He wanted to rein in her pain.

Does it hurt?

She groaned.

He reached down to stroke her face, and said, You really are hurting. Don't bite off your tongue.

Unh.

With pain like this, you'll remember Big Daddy for the rest of your life.

Unh.

When Big Daddy—got money—he'll come—make you—hurt—hurt—hurt! When he's got enough money, Big Daddy'll take you home and marry you, so you can take the hurt nice and slow.

After the event she completely forgot him. One day, a man came in and thunked a bag of money on the table. The table was lame to begin with, and one leg slipped.

He said, I said I'd come and marry you, and here I am!

Fusang said, Here you are.

I was really worried you wouldn't be able to wait so long, that you'd go off with someone else. You weren't getting worried?

No. Will you have jasmine or oolong, sir?

You don't know what kind of tea I drink?

We've only got jasmine and oolong.

You don't remember me? I told you I'd rob, steal, or kill to get you out of here! He went up and grabbed her by the chin. Take a good look at me!

It's you, all right.

I went to sea! Others get forced to; I went of my own free will! For you! Do you know how dangerous it is? Nine out of ten sailors die out there!

Fusang took the sailor over to the cashier.

Calculated on the basis of her daily consumption of a catty of rice and two-fifths of a catty of shrimp, the price of her redemption ended up fifty dollars over what the man had. And that was cheap, considering what a glutton she was.

He agreed to come back the next day with enough to pay for all the rice and shrimp Fusang had eaten over five hundred and ninety days, and, as long as he was at it, to hire a palanquin, borrow a bridal headdress, and buy two strings of firecrackers.

The man who arrived bright and early the next morning tossed a bag of money at the cashier, who knew at a glance there was no need to count it.

He had brought along a makeshift wedding canopy. With a tug here and a pull there it was ready.

The man dragged Fusang under the canopy, where they stood facing each other and then knelt side by side. When he didn't come up again after the first kowtow, Fusang discovered he had just been killed from behind.

The killer pulled out the hatchet and came toward her, holding it above his head. He would have killed her too, if everyone in the yard hadn't come running. As he was pulled away, the killer stamped his foot at Fusang:

Yesterday I was short a little rice and fish money and today you go off with somebody else! You wait two whole years, and then change your mind overnight?

Everybody urged him to look at it this way. The poor sap who just got chopped in the back had been waiting three years.

Fusang was truly bewildered; she couldn't remember waiting for anyone.

Still refusing to surrender his hatchet, the man said he now knew why whores were called fickle and faithless.

The others said, Don't say that, we're all whores here.

What do you call something that goes whichever way the wind blows, that knows no laws of human decency? A whore, that's what!

Come on, sir, calm down, it's not so easy being a whore either, you know. Cajoling him the whole way, they threw him out the door.

But it wasn't over. Shortly afterward a whole gang of men showed up looking for the killer. He tried to steal our brother's bride, right in the middle of the wedding! They vowed to chop him to pieces and boil him alive.

That same day, notices of the challenge were plastered all over Chinatown. Before long, another gang of men on horseback appeared, pasting acceptance notices right next to them. Not long after that, both sides put up battle announcements, in which, after several adjustments, the day was set for the following spring when the plum trees bloomed, because hatchets and cleavers are hard to wield convincingly in winter clothes, and because both sides wanted more time to practice.

When the plum trees bloomed, they made a further adjustment. Since only half the weapons were ready, how about pushing it back another couple of months?

Both sides assigned men to watch over the only smithy in the city. They kept him up at night. He doubled his price, reconsidered, and then doubled it again. He'd get baked to a crisp but grow rich in the process. Once he finished the job, he would rent another parcel of land to add to his ranch outside the city. For a time there, all the cutlers on the three streets of Chinatown were completely out of stock. If anyone came looking for the blacksmith, the men from both camps would drive him away. He's working on cleavers that will slaughter men. He's got no time for your chickens and pigs.

The weapons were finally finished. News compounded daily and with it people's interest. The white devils were just as excited as everyone else and had already gone out to choose the best spots for watching the fight.

In the gambling houses, saloons, and brothels, one frequently heard arguments over which side would win. Every day someone would tell Fusang the latest, but nobody connected the event with her, the dutiful whore without a quarrel with the world.

She didn't know the reason behind the fight. She never knew how many men had fought to the death over her. Whenever a fight broke out in her room, she quietly stepped aside, grabbing a handful of melon seeds on her way. When the men had beaten one another bloody and knocked out each other's teeth, they would ask her, Who do you like the best?

That put her in a bind. Weren't they all the same? She'd reply with a smile, I like you both.

But who's your favorite?

She'd just smile at them both in exactly the same way.

Then they'd start beating her.

She felt she'd done nothing wrong and besides, the result would be the same no matter which one she picked. If she'd said she liked this one, that one would beat her, and far worse than the two of them beating her together. Two sharing the task of beating her was like two monks carrying a bucket of water, each shirking a bit, each relying on the other. Though Fusang wasn't a clever girl, at the grand old age of twenty-two, this much she knew.

She couldn't remember how many men she'd had— white or yellow, gentle or rough—none of them gave her any reason to remember him. They liked to be remembered by whores, but Fusang could strain her mind to the itching point and still not remember a soul.

Except for the little white devil named Chris. However she turned away from him, she still knew those pale blue eyes were upon her.

No one had ever told Fusang about the age-old trap called love.

At daybreak, footsteps and hoofbeats could be heard outside.

ONLY WITH THE BREAK OF DAY did Chris realize he had been searching through the night. A lone building stood at the end of a dead-end street. The lower part of the windows were bricked and boarded up, leaving a crack a hand's width at the very top, its darkness arresting in the dawn light. This was the hospital everyone shuddered to mention.

Chris tethered his horse and surveyed the building. It was a converted warehouse, designed to keep anyone on the outside from figuring out what went on inside. No one could climb to such high windows, or even if they could there was no way to see through those cracks. The door was locked with a lock far too big for it.

Chris rolled an oil drum up from the corner. The street was on a hill; after every few revolutions, he had to stop, catch his breath, and straighten his undershirt, which was bunched and twisted and soaked with sweat.

A Chinese man was lighting a stove outside his door. He stared at Chris in bewilderment for a while and then called out to a few others who joined him in that activity.

There was a group of people outside another house. They were workers just off the night shift at the cigar factory. Chris didn't know that they were waiting for beds, that they couldn't go to bed until those inside had gotten up. They ignored him, for they were already asleep, squatting on their heels like a row of birds perched on a branch.

Chris finally got the oil drum up the hill. The wind

was much stronger there and it took a lot of effort to stand the drum on end under a window.

Chris stood on the drum, but still couldn't reach the crack at the top of the window. Then he remembered his little mirror. He raised it to the crack and adjusted the angle. Ever since he was a little boy, he had liked looking at unusual things with it: baby foxes suckling, the cook picking her nose while a hired man stuck his hand up her skirt, birds kissing, the feet of his siblings and cousins kicking each other under the dining room table. In this mirror, he had even seen his aunt give birth to his youngest girl cousin.

He patiently rotated his wrist and suddenly he could see everything.

YOU DRIFT UP FROM THE DAZE of shallow sleep to see a circle of white light moving across your pillow and the wall beside your bed. You look at me, wondering if this is what awakened you.

I just got back from the square where two armies fought over you more than a hundred years ago. Of course, you don't know they were fighting over you. You have to wait a hundred years, for someone like me to dig through one hundred and sixty history books, the way the Chinese kept chipping away in the most depleted gold mines, for the truth to finally pan out. All accounts of the fight are pretty vague. They say things like: "Allegedly it had something to do with a prostitute," and "Allegedly that prostitute was the cause of the conflict." I don't use the word *allegedly*, I just say, It was you. You were the cause of it all.

No need for such alarm. You can't be held responsible for all the wars waged through the ages over women. Waging war over women—especially a woman as beautiful and undiscriminating toward men as you—has got to be one of the best pretexts for war there is, for every war must have its pretext. Compared with fighting and killing for oil, for politics, for a bunch of people you don't even know but take to be your leaders, or even for peace, fighting over you seems far more genuine. So what do you have to be sorry about?

The circle of white light is coming in through the crack at the top of the window. It falls on your face, your hair, your neck. It is not from the lantern of the Customs devils. I'm fed up with them too. The INS has been just plain mean for over a hundred years now. How can you think the man stationed at Customs in international airports and the Big Beard who once guarded the dock aren't one and the same?

The white light has now stopped at your bedside, where it shines on a bowl half full of rice, your last meal before death. You reach out your hand, pick up a grain of rice, and put it in your mouth. Before long, the rice becomes the heat now tingling through your body. But you're still too weak to wonder how this circle of light got in or what it is.

Your vision gradually grows clearer. Now you manage to get out of bed and follow the bright round thing. A big centipede is hanging in the air; at closer range you see that it is climbing up a hank of black hair. The hair is hanging down from the top bunk, and you trace it to a head, a face. There has been somebody else in here with you all along. The circle of light stops on her head. This companion of yours is dead. Dead but keeping you company the whole time. She has been dead for some time now; it seems to me she has even begun to melt a bit. But you believe she hasn't been dead long at all, for a bowl lies tipped beside her face, and the drops of tea that had dripped through the bed planks onto your face—you felt she had sent them to call out to you, to make conversation with you.

The centipede has completed its climb at last, stopping half in the black hair, half on the waxen yellow forehead. Don't you dare touch it or I'll puke... .You pick it up by the tail. Caught in the white light, it squirms and struggles. You drop it on the floor and squash it, knowing it would come crawling back, next time toward you.

You notice your dead companion has half a bowl of rice beside her too. You lift the bowl to your lips and scrape the rice into your mouth in two swipes. You are not like her, feeling so wronged by these circumstances as to rashly refuse to eat. The rice was so dry it may as well have been raw, and now each little grain is standing on end in your belly, but you don't care.

You see it—that's the door. The circle of light is moving back and forth between it and your feet. You are sure this white light is your own soul wanting to go out.

When you fall, your hand almost catches the door-knob. Never mind, it is locked from the outside anyway. I'm going to stop describing your surroundings to look at your unconscious face. You no longer know anything. You don't know that Chris is now using his little mirror to look up and down your face, which is resting on your left arm. You just look like you are sleeping.

After a moment he has an idea, jumps down from the oil drum, and unhitches his horse. All I can tell is that his haste must have something to do with a plan he has. But I have no idea what it is. When it comes to the thinking of white people, guessing is pointless. Whether you bother to try and guess or not, something unexpected is bound to happen anyway.

Let me take this opportunity while you are unconscious to reread another passage about the battle over you: "The warriors arrived at four o'clock in the afternoon. Their white silk garments bulged over cleavers and hatchets. Reporters from the morning and afternoon papers lined the square; when they asked whether a famous prostitute was behind the fight, no one would answer. . . ."

Someone must be coming for you, because footsteps have stopped outside your door.

You don't move. You have no reaction at all to the sound of the door unlocking.

THE DOOR OPENED in the afternoon. Four men came in and stood there in silence, looking at Fusang, who had nearly crawled right out the door. None of the others had ever made it so far. The most any of them had done was crawl over to the wall, where they managed to loop their sash over a wooden clothes peg. None had succeeded in hanging herself.

One of the men put his hand under Fusang's nose and said, Almost. Another hour ought to do it.

Another said, Let's take that one first. She died minding her manners.

Let's take both together! She's just a breath away anyway, isn't she?

Yeah. Let's finish her off with the rope and take both of them together, save ourselves a trip.

The rope? Fuck. What if she bites my hand?

Listen to her belly—she's got a whole opera going on in there.

Then it's any minute now. That's just a few last farts before she dies. Hand me the rope.

Fusang parted her lips and said, Don't strangle me.

The four of them jumped back. Looked at one another. The one nearest Fusang said, Then what do you suggest?

Fusang sighed and mumbled, but they couldn't hear a word she said. They gestured to one another with their eyes: Ignore her. Strangle her and get it over with.

It's for your own good, do you hear me? Quick and easy, you won't feel a thing.

Hurry the fuck up! I hear someone coming!

It's those white devils who just asked for directions. I'm not strangling her now. . . .

You motherfucker, give me that rope. Time's running out!

The slipknot went over Fusang's head and started to tighten when it reached her jaw. She caught it on her chin as she gasped for breath.

Too late! They'll be here any minute!

The men shoved Fusang back inside.

Lock the door! We'll finish her off when they leave.

They went outside and snuck around the side of the building, planted their feet, and wound their queues on top of their heads, watching three white devils run to the front and look around. They heard hoofbeats in the distance.

Chris, is this the place?

Yes, I just saw them locking the door.

Look! Two old foreigner ladies. Are they missionaries?

At least it's not the cops.

What are they saying, Chris?

I don't understand it. I bet they've got the key!

That little white devil is a spy—people saw him lurking around here before dawn.

Hello, please open the door!

We're from the Rescue Society. Please open this door at once.

No English. No understand.

The little white devil is whispering in their ears.

Get a good look at that little devil's face—one of these days I'm going to break his kneecaps.

Chris, said one of the women, are you sure this is the place?

Absolutely. Should I go borrow an ax?

Will those foreign missionary ladies call the cops?

Looks to me like she wants to set the place on fire. What's that they've got over their nose and mouth?

It's called a face mask.

You think they won't set the place on fire? Last time they burned eight Chinese houses, said they were killing rats!

Lord forgive them who speak such a vile language! Chinese is the ugliest language I've ever heard. Did Chris get the ax?

Yes, here he comes now . . .

They wouldn't lend me one!

Tell them we will open this door with or without a key.

What are they saying, can you tell?

Those ladies from the Rescue Society want to break the door in.

What's a rescue society?

They put themselves in charge of meddling in our business. You punish a little whore by telling her to get down on her knees, they meddle; you buy a whore and sell her again to make a little money, and they meddle in that! Every last one of these little whores was sold by her own parents—who's to say we can't sell them too?

That damned mission just opened last year and they kidnapped dozens of whores in the first month.

What an ugly language!

It's the Lord's will, Mary, we're not here to save their language!

The little white devil's got a big rock!

Smash it, smash it!

Dorothy, they're armed. . . .

Harder, Chris, harder!

We're asking for trouble, Dorothy, this is yellow territory!

Yellow territory? Over my dead body! Here, Chris, let me try.

Dorothy, let's call the police! They're four men!

The San Francisco Police have made it quite clear they will no longer intervene in matters between the Chinese.

Stop! This is our property!

Didn't you say you don't speak English?

Leave that lock alone! Or we're calling the cops.

Did you hear that? They're calling the cops! Chris, take over, hurry!

Damn. They've just about got it open. Come on, we've got to stop them!

At this point the hoofbeats from the bottom of the hill were drawing closer. Everyone turned to look.

A dark shadow splashed over the ground like dirty water, arriving long before the person making it appeared.

People could see the setting sun under the belly of his horse.

The lock fell to the ground and the door opened with a cawing sound. The shape of the woman lying inside gradually surfaced through the darkness.

Oh my God! Lord above! Chris, quick, cover your nose!

You foreigners are forbidden to enter! This is a Chinese hospital!

We are foreigners?!

Take your hands off me! You call this a hospital? For shame that such a hospital should exist in our land! I could die of shame!

If you take one step further we're. . .calling the cops!

Be my guest! By all means, call the cops!

Keep out!

Chris, here's a handkerchief, cover your nose!

Let them go in, said the man on horseback. Let them cover their noses and rescue us all.

The Chinese watched him dismount. His face was still hidden by his wide-brimmed calfskin Stetson. Something flashed—not his eyes, but the teeth in his smile. He wore four rings on each hand and gold clips on his pant legs. The four men wondered where such shiny precious things could have come from.

When they came closer, they remembered the Ah Ding who had disappeared so long ago, and the Da Yong rumored to have recently emerged.

One of them said, We thought you died.

He said, So did I.

By this point, the white devils were carrying Fusang away.

Where are you taking her?

Out of this hell!

Da Yong watched in bemusement as the missionaries fluttered over Fusang like a pair of angels, and as the little white devil with the pale blue eyes stared first at the hospital, then at the four men, and finally at Da Yong himself. Grinning, he pulled out a plug of chewing tobacco, put it in his mouth, and slowly began to chew.

The Rescue Society's shabby hansom creaked into motion.

THIS IS THE FIRST TIME you've combed your hair in a month. You are sitting up and your dead brittle hair covers the floor. New growth has begun beneath your scalp and your head itches all over. You made it. As you turn your neck back and forth in the morning light, I can see your shrunken ears. In fact, it wasn't medicine that saved you. You knew you weren't going to die when you stole the rice from the corpse. That's how I knew I could safely leave you and go see how preparations for the fight were progressing. Did anyone still remember you were the pretext for it? Later I realized that they no longer needed one. No one cared where you were by then.

The only point of interest in your sterile white room was a spiderweb. For the month you lay in that white bed, you focused all your desire to disrupt the whiteness on that spiderweb. But one day someone broke it with a broom, and the whiteness was whole once more.

Their fingers were as white as the stripped roots of trees. They pinched your nose and stuck white tablets down your throat. One day you smiled at them, grabbed the pills, put them in your mouth, and chewed them up like fried soy beans. They stared at you, not sure whether to laugh or run.

Chris came to see you once a week. Between his punctual arrival and punctual departure, he sat in the chair in the corner. One day you changed out of the baggy white sackcloth into your own form-fitting wrinkled red satin blouse. Chris walked in the door and was terrified by the stark red. Instead of the chair in the corner, he headed straight toward you, as if in a dream.

You leaned against the bed rail with an encouraging smile, as if watching a child who had just learned to walk. He came right up to you and stood just a foot away, like the first time he saw you at twelve. He had something important to say and you waited. But time ran out.

The old missionary named Mary appeared in the doorway. You and Chris were standing beside the bed. She understood what was happening better than you and Chris did. She was appalled. How could you whore *here*, she asked, how could you seduce a child?

Chris suddenly understood.

Lifting your heavy lashes, you looked at Mary and then

at Chris. Mary interpreted your calm innocence as shamelessness. Chris never imagined that you would react by doing absolutely nothing, as if you had been so shameless for so long that Mary's words could not hurt you at all.

Her colorless lips were still flapping. She said she could no longer allow you anywhere near this boy. Have you no conscience? she asked. Look at him, he's only fourteen! She tossed the sackcloth at you and said, That red thing you're wearing is a filthy sin.

The red blouse was crumpled up and thrown in the trash. Late that night you stole down the stairs and groped through the garbage to retrieve it. You tenaciously believed that it and it alone would allow Chris to recognize the real you.

Chris stopped coming. But you never stopped thinking about what hadn't happened. What it was, deep down, you knew. You secretly waited for him to grow up, to treat you as a grown man would. Yet you knew he would be like no other man.

At first, you didn't even know you were waiting for him. You combed your hair languidly, watching the people and horses go by on the street. Without moving at all, you went everywhere looking for him. Finally, you really saw him standing across the street, looking right at you.

When your eyes met, you halted the comb in midstroke and smiled at him. But he turned away. He started kicking at a cobblestone. Once he dislodged it, he kicked it back and forth. He seemed to want to set himself against something and everything seemed set against him. He couldn't even bother to hide his childishness.

You waited as his gaze climbed inch by inch up the building to your window the way he had climbed the tree that time. When his eyes finally reached you, you met them as if taking him into your arms.

When he felt you take him in, he stood stock still. His childishness vanished.

From then on, you went to the window facing the street at that same time every day. He was never there. Yet for an instant, everyone on the street would become him.

Let me tell you what is wrong with what you're feeling, the thing that makes us laugh at the very mention of the word: Love. Really. The word itself smells funny to us, like milk gone bad. We came to this country mouthing through gritted teeth, Freedom, Get rich, Sex. If someone were to blurt out, I love you, what do you think we would do? What else could we do but laugh? Laughter takes care of numbness, bashfulness, and an instinct that has faded from memory. That instinct, passed from you to me, from our ancestors to the present, is the longing for love. At least you can see how busy I am; we're so much busier nowadays, busy enough to lose that instinct entirely. When we truly can stand it no longer, we go off to the movies and watch two-dimensional people love to death and live to love, and we return to three dimensions re-lieved, rejoicing, thankful such love does not exist in the real world.

I shake my head in dismay because you have fallen into that age-old trap called love.

You don't realize that Chris has been avoiding showing up across the street at the same time as before. He rides ten miles on his horse, letting the ocean winds blow his face raw, simply to come here for a glimpse of your empty window. He needs this torture. It makes no difference to a fourteen-year-old boy whether the window is empty or not.

You have no idea that he went to the newspapers to tell what he had seen with his very own eyes at the hospital for Chinese prostitutes. He said it was the worst hell on earth. He described the tooth and nail marks on the beds, the bloodstains on the walls, the termite damage to the floors. The reporters were forced to slacken the clacking of their typewriters and wait for him to get hold of himself and recapture the thread of his tale. He would conclude by vowing to do anything to wipe out those yellow slave owners. When he used the word *rescue,* the expression on his face was adorable, because it took him back to the adventure stories of his childhood.

How could you know how much he hated Chinese men? As he walked alone through the tawdry streets of Chinatown, every single man with a queue was someone who hurt you. He believed that if those men were gone, all your troubles would disappear. You were beautiful and kind, and you would be free. What he could not anticipate, though, was the fact that if those men disappeared, so would you.

Thanks to Chris, photographs and stories of the hospital made the pages of several different papers. Whites, friend and foe of the Chinese alike, shuddered to think such an eyesore could exist on American soil.

Chris did it all for you.

He could not have expected that he would no longer bite his lip and walk away in a cold sweat at the sight of violence against the Chinese. He had changed. He would halt his horse and squeeze his way through a crowd to watch dispassionately as five or six Chinese men got strung up by their queues. Even a guy bragging about the belt he wore, woven from a Chinaman's queue, failed to disgust him much. Standing at the pasture fence on his father's ranch, watching a group of men drive out their only Chinese neighbor, he was thinking of the word *rescue*.

You are now staying in your first place of rescue, a white building too clean to tolerate even the smallest spiderweb. Your room is on the top floor, to quarantine you, but also to keep you from corrupting the girls who have already been reformed.

Please move a little closer here, so I can see the downy new growth at your hairline and how your face is filling out.

Out your back window, rows of girls in the courtyard downstairs are singing. They all have the same short haircut, for lice control. You know the singing will be followed by long prayers. And then everybody will go to the table for a bowl of soup and a piece of bread.

Frowning, you imagine yourself becoming like them and laugh.

There are three rows of girls and the wind blows identical ripples through their identical gray cotton dresses.

They flutter in the breeze for quite some time. The missionary named Dorothy walks over. She is a fine young woman, pretty and kind.

Arms crossed over her chest, she says, Girls, something terrible has happened. You can't tell whether she is saddened or embarrassed.

She pauses and says, My children, how could you do such a thing?

Along with the girls downstairs, you crane your neck. What could have happened to hurt Dorothy like this?

Mary bellows, Say no more! Let them see for themselves!

You watch the girls darting their eyes around them in distress as they follow Mary and Dorothy inside. Twenty-four pairs of identical feet trudge up the stairs. Nothing the girls did had ever made the missionaries so mad before, not even wasting half a piece of bread or sneaking over to the walls around the mission yard to indulge in the colorful sounds of the filthy Chinese spoken outside. Whatever happened must have been terrible, you decide.

You lean out over the railing to look down the stairwell. The girls are standing outside the largest bedroom.

My dear children, Dorothy says, I simply cannot believe . . .

At this point two girls come out with a metal pail. Mary

trains her eyes on the twenty-four girls from behind her glasses. One of them had come into your room one day and asked you, Just been rescued?

You said yes.

She said, I've been a student here for ages. You've got to study a long time before you learn how to be good.

What is this? Mary asks, pointing to the pail, the very tip of her finger disgusted.

You prop your chin in your hands and keep watching.

Not one of the twenty-four girls moves or says a word.

Mary says, Who did this?

Dorothy repeats the question.

Mary says, This is not the doing of one or two girls. Is there any among you who cannot find her way to the privy? Or who feels the privy is too far to walk? How can you use the bedroom to. . .to relieve yourselves? I guess some people just prefer to live in a toilet or to turn any sort of place into one!

The girls return to the courtyard. You remain just as you were, your elbows resting on the railing. You hear Mary say, I realize some things are just impossible to re-form, like these creatures possessed by the devil.

You hear weeping and through it her faltering words, Those Chinese. . .punish us all when they bring girls like this into the world.

You feel there's no great need to understand every word of that sort of talk.

. . .

A GROUP OF CHINESE MEN in black Stetsons stopped at the peeling grille of the mission door and looked around. They said with their eyes, This is the place. Shall we? Okay, let's do it.

One rang the doorbell. Five minutes went by and no one answered.

The man who rang the doorbell said, They're probably hiding her right now, Da Yong.

Ring again.

Da Yong, they just get more and more sneaky. By now those missionaries can lie and preach Scripture with the same straight face.

Ring it again. Da Yong tidied his queue and tossed it over his shoulder. He told his six men, Take down your queues or they'll think we're here to snatch her.

What *are* we here for?

Da Yong smirked. To snatch her.

The door opened a crack and an old doorman looked out at them, then back over his shoulder, and asked, What do you want?

We're looking for. . .Just in time, Da Yong whacked the man who had started to answer on the back of the head and took over, We're looking for a girl called Ah Fu. He clasped his hat to his chest and bowed excessively.

The doorman closed the door and went off. The men turned to Da Yong in bewilderment: Where had this Ah Fu come from?

Da Yong put on his hat, lining up the center of the

brim with his nose, leaving himself nearly cross-eyed with the effort. By asking for Ah Fu, he had ensured that the missionaries would hide only her. Ah Fu was the pharmacist's twelve-year-old daughter-in-law, engaged to help raise and then marry his infant son. She had been suddenly rescued by the missionaries one day and brought to the reform school, still carrying the two ounces of pickled duck tongue she'd just bought for the pharmacist. Da Yong kept a mental tally of all the rescued girls.

The young missionary appeared and looked at Da Yong and the others with disdain. Ah Fu? We have no such name on our roster.

Then who do you have on your roster? Da Yong grinned, and stared at her exquisite neck, his eyes still somewhat crossed.

She felt she had been offended somehow. The names on our roster are none of your concern.

Right, Da Yong said.

Describe her, please, she said to him.

With a nearly imperceptible forward tilt to his head, Da Yong hunched his shoulders slightly, his whole body now the picture of doltish timidity. This kept Dorothy from recognizing him as the bejeweled kingpin on horseback from two months ago. He spoke pure pidgin English, casting his eyes this way and that as he racked every corner of his brain to come up with a word. This was an old trick of his, to make his adversaries underestimate him. The best part of it was, if the thing ever got hauled into court, he could always use the language barrier to get off.

Relaxing her guard somewhat, Dorothy said, Okay. She took in the size of the group and said, Only two of you can come in.

Da Yong said, Thank you, miss. Turning to the others, he said, The lady says two of you have to stay out here and the rest of us can go in.

Before Dorothy could correct him, five of them had pushed through the door.

All twenty-four girls in the classroom stopped what they were doing when they saw Da Yong and his men. The girls were sitting around a long table with a stack of Bible pages in front of them. They spent four hours a day binding them, four reading and copying them, and another two singing from them.

Almost no one had ever succeeded in reclaiming a girl from the mission. The building had a secret passage, and no sooner was a girl's name announced at the front door than she was already being hidden away. There was only one time, when two men got in pretending to be plumbers and then whipped out a chain, that the missionaries could do nothing but watch as they made off with an eleven-year-old girl.

Dorothy followed Da Yong with her eyes as he stopped at each of the twenty-four faces before moving on to the next and then back again.

Did you find her? she asked.

Da Yong said nothing. Of course the girl he was looking for wasn't there.

Then I must see you out, Dorothy said.

Thank you. Da Yong let himself be escorted from the classroom.

The door is to your right, Dorothy said.

Da Yong said to his men, The door is to the left.

The men turned and climbed the staircase to the left.

Dorothy was stunned and Da Yong joined her in that reaction.

On the top floor, the men shouted as they subdued Fusang. They tied the chain around her wrists and neck, jerked it tight, and fastened the lock. The clanking could be heard all the way downstairs.

When she saw Da Yong at the door, Fusang started to open her mouth, as recall half-surfaced, then froze.

Da Yong said, That was really quite rude of you to empty out my jewelry case like that.

Fusang's gaze slowly fell to her feet. Her bun had been yanked loose and her hair was a mess.

Mary called over a tall girl to translate and told her, Don't leave out a single word.

Dorothy walked up to Fusang and said, Don't worry, we know he's lying. She turned to Da Yong, That's the biggest lie on earth. We saved her life!

Da Yong yanked Fusang over to him with one hand and punched her in the face with the other. Dorothy could do nothing to save her now.

Another punch threw Fusang against the wall.

The missionaries cried out in alarm and covered their faces, refusing to watch such barbarity.

Don't be mad, Da Yong said to Fusang softly, I took off my rings first. He hit her again, and said, Look, you haven't lost a single tooth. He turned to the missionaries: I'm hitting her for you as well—she's probably stolen a lot of your stuff too. He made to punch her again.

Stop! Dorothy shouted, For God's sake, stop!

Mary shouted, Hitting is not allowed! You animal!

Ask her if hitting is allowed or not, Da Yong said, pointing to Fusang. Look, she doesn't mind. He turned to Fusang and said, Don't worry, I won't knock you out.

No more hitting! Stop it!

She's a born thief, Da Yong said as he continued punching Fusang. Bind her hands and she'll steal with her feet!

No one noticed Chris standing right outside, watching through the partly open door and the gaps between all the heads in the crowd as Fusang took punch after punch.

Da Yong stopped, straightened his hat and clothes, and said to his men, Okay, take her away.

Dorothy said, You can't!

Mary said, You are not taking anyone out of this school.

Da Yong said, It's an old Chinese custom; the thief belongs to the one he stole from.

We never saw her steal anything!

Do you have any evidence?

Da Yong expressed his understanding for their motherly good intentions, then said with a sneer, Good-bye. When we get back, we'll take our time and beat the evidence out of her.

If you really must take her, then I'm going with you.

Da Yong looked at the young saint who had shown such courage, smiled as if through a headache, and said, Oh no, miss, our place is so crowded even the dog has to wag his tail up and down.

Don't think you can stop me. Mary, please bring me my hat and gloves. I'm going. We rescued this sister and I'd believe her over you any day! I will stand by her side and I won't back down until you show me some evidence. I will not believe she is a thief unless I hear it from her own lips.

With a sweep of his arm, Da Yong said, Take her and let's go. Don't tell me she's gotten to you? These foreign biddies couldn't kill an ant if they tried! When his men continued to hesitate, he roared, Fuck your old mothers and death to your whole clans!

Mary said to the girl who was translating, Tell me what he just said, word for word.

Da Yong said to the girl, Do it and I'll be back to make chop suey out of you.

One of the men started tightening the chain around Fusang's wrists.

Young Dorothy calmly held out her arms and planted herself like a crucifix in Fusang's path.

Da Yong said, Just push her out of the way. Let's go!

Chris noticed Fusang looking at him. The expression on her face was one of total uninvolvement, as if she had no idea what everyone was fighting about. She licked a trickle of blood from her cheek with all the detachment of a bystander.

Then everyone heard her say, I'm a thief. I'll go with you.

Everything stopped.

Fusang said, I took his jewelry.

She bowed her head and smiled deeply to herself.

Chris was the only one to see a faint impression of satisfaction in her smile.

A FEW YEARS LATER Chris would come to understand that smile.

It suddenly came back to him one morning when he was seventeen: So that's what it was. He was on a steamship and had come to understand that many things just couldn't be helped, which is simply to say he was growing up. It's a sign of maturity to admit it when something is hopeless. Chris finally understood that heartfelt smile of Fusang's.

She really *had* been smiling to herself.

Before the smile, she had said, I'm a thief. I'll go with you. I took his jewelry. She hadn't expected to say this. But when she smiled that way, she realized what she was. She understood then that it was her nature to steal pleasure from suffering.

Or perhaps that idea had occurred to her as long back as the day she'd reclaimed her true self by putting on that red blouse. Chris was just like all men—the version of her they were drawn to was the one in red.

On that morning at seventeen, Chris recalled the first time he'd entered that sterile white room, how when he saw her leaning against the headboard, wearing that monastic white sackcloth and smiling at him, he had not moved any closer. Suddenly, they were strangers. He sat in the chair in the corner, telling himself with all his might, This is Fusang, an Oriental prostitute as beautiful and charming as temptation itself. But it didn't work. His obsession with her was gone.

She seemed to sense the change in him. She undid her braid and languidly toyed with the ends of her hair.

He had no desire to move closer to her. He loved her just the same, but distance now seemed both proper and necessary.

Chris stayed for half an hour that time. In the days following, he made straight for the chair in the corner, as if on business. He had to keep telling himself, This is someone whose life I saved. She's getting better every day. Sometimes it would occur to him, So what am I doing here? There was no longer anything special between them, thanks to the white sackcloth. He gradually shortened his visits. Thirty minutes. Twenty. Ten.

The day he finally decided his visits weren't doing either of them any good, he climbed the stairs listening to twenty-odd girls singing through their mouths without involving any deeper parts of themselves. When he found Fusang's door partly open, he reached out to knock, but his hand stopped in midair. When he opened the door wider, he saw her body, wrapped in soft red cloth, turn to him.

Sitting before a cracked mirror the size of a *wutong* leaf, Fusang turned to look at him. The soiled crimson stung him and he felt all his senses shift. Even remembering the moment three years later, his senses experienced that same shift coursing through his whole body. He was as stunned as he had been the first time he saw her.

She cut a swath of red through the suffocating whiteness. The red bled into the whiteness like ink on rice paper.

Her hand was fastening her remaining earring. The hand fell still, but the earring wouldn't.

Step by step, he walked toward her. This time he knew this wasn't all there was to it, that it wouldn't stop here, that each step entailed a next step, that even when he had collapsed all distance between them, there would still be another next step.

There could have been many next steps. That morning at seventeen, Chris retraced each one of them in detail.

The next step could have been to take yet another step when there was nowhere farther to go and walk right into her.

He could have said, Come away with me. Be my mistress, the way all the men in my family have mistresses. This was another next step.

Or he could have solemnly embraced her and solemnly branded an oath upon her lips. Without needing to say a word, all he had to do was pull off his necklace, the one his mother had given him, take Fusang's hand, and press the locket into her palm, as if placing the final piece on a chessboard.

Chris thought, that morning at seventeen, that whichever next step he took would have set in motion an unknowable future; each next step shows you its own even more unpredictable next step. He remembered clearly the way Fusang's hands had come to rest on his shoulders, on his face just shaven for the first time. The red flushed the very air around her.

Just as Chris at fourteen was standing before Fusang's red blouse, aware of all those next steps, the door had flung open and slammed against the wall.

What followed was Mary's tirade, which hit like collapsing bricks.

Fusang was a wild beast in red, Chris the prey lured to her maw. You see, events could also entail this sort of next step. Events could be understood this way too, in the mind of a missionary from a rescue society for girls.

Chris watched as Fusang just stared wide-eyed in bewilderment, taking in the righteousness quivering wildly in the missionary's gray eyes as she shouted and crossed herself. Chris came to feel she was right; he shouldn't get close to this prostitute, especially not in this room so pure and white it was sacred.

Afterward, he went to Fusang's window often, but then avoided seeing her. The window was just as satisfying without her.

On that morning at seventeen, Chris also recalled the scene of Fusang's capture, how she was jerked about by the chain, how her blood spattered the walls. He had nearly charged through the door, picked up the chair in the corner, and gone after those men in queues with everything he had. And then Fusang suddenly saw him there. Looking right over all the commotion in the room, she signaled to him with her eyes. It was as if the two of them had a secret plan and she was reminding him not to forget it. Maybe neither of them knew what it was, just that they had one, solid enough to keep them from letting on or having to deal with anyone else. His rage left him and the two of them formed a bond across the room. It now occurred to Chris, at seventeen, that it was as if they had made the commitment to run away together.

And then the missionaries had tried to stop them from taking her, using their bodies and souls as shields. Evidence! You can't take her without evidence. . . .

I'm a thief. I'll go with you. At that critical moment, Fusang had spoken.

If she wanted to leave the white room, she must have been a thief.

Perhaps she had started thinking about leaving when

Mary yelled at her. Or maybe it was when they threw her red blouse in the trash.

Chris finally understood what had happened that day. Dragged off in chains by a gang of men, her face bloody, her hair a mess, Fusang had become a typical slave girl. Yet she had bowed her head and smiled to herself.

How absurd! At thirty, at forty, for the rest of his life, Chris would keep thinking of the way Fusang smiled. Whether you set her free or enslaved her, her freedom came completely from within. But this was too hard for him to understand at fourteen. He watched Fusang walk out the door and climb into the carriage.

He would always remember the slave owner named Da Yong, whose face made a mockery of the whole world, Come whoring again soon, little mister.

Chris said, Sooner or later you're going to hell.

Thank you, you little shit. With one last grin, Da Yong had leapt into the carriage.

BY THE TIME CHRIS GOT HOME it was midnight. He had just taken off his boots when a servant came up and said, Your father's waiting for you.

His father had dozed off in his chair in the living room. His glasses had slipped to the end of his steep nose as if dangling over a cliff. Chris could have righted them, but didn't. He didn't want to do anything to curry favor with his father at a time like this. He didn't want to exhibit any behavior that seemed like an attempt to win his father over, lest his father form the mistaken impression that he hoped to avoid the conversation they were about to have.

He knew things did not look good. A fourteen-year-old boy who had skipped classes, stayed out late, broken his father's rules—he wouldn't get off lightly this time. But he wouldn't confess. Silence was allowed in his family; all those secret interracial affairs depended on it.

Silence keeps one honest. Honesty builds self-respect. If you can't tell the truth, keep your mouth shut. So his father once said. He had just returned from the South. He didn't discuss the war with anyone but his brother. As far as he was concerned, life and death, and courage and cruelty, were completely different for those who had never experienced war. People who had never been to war didn't even deserve to hear about it. At first, when people kept asking him about it, he would sigh, smile wearily, and say a few things. By the time Chris started to take an interest in the war, everyone in the family was used to his father's silence on the subject. They all pretended to know nothing about the black girl he'd kept in his tent.

When his father woke up, his glasses fell on the book of poetry in his lap and then bounced to the floor and broke. Ignoring them, he looked straight at Chris. There was no transition from sleep to wakefulness; he was alert the instant he opened his eyes.

Have you been waiting long? his father asked.

Yes, Chris replied.

I won't apologize, for I've been waiting longer, his father said.

Chris kept looking at him.

May I know why you made me stay up waiting for you to come home? Do I have that right?

Yes, sir.

A long silence. Which included his father ringing for a servant and waiting for him to pick up the broken eyeglasses from the floor. Then his father picked up his cigar cutter and snipped the ash of the cigar by the ashtray. Lighting up, he said, Well? Which meant the interrogation had not been interrupted after all.

Chris told him about the demonstration in the city, tens of thousands of people demanding the government drive out the coolies, and the mission rescuing Chinese slave girls. One of them was dragged off in chains today—

His father suddenly interrupted him, Look at your hands, how you keep clutching at your trousers. All right, you may continue.

He knew his father wanted to stop his lies. Or his half-truths.

He realized how stupid he was for rattling on like that.

From now on, his father said, five minutes after his previous remark, you are forbidden to ride your horse. Until this secret of yours—I have no way of knowing what it is, but it is the reason you keep going into the city—is completely dead. I too have secrets, many, many secrets, but they all die sooner or later and get replaced by new secrets. So will yours. After a time you will find yourself smiling and fretting over some new secret. And that secret won't be as bad as this one, because this one has now reached the crisis point, as far as I can tell. How old are you, Chris?

Chris weighed his father doubtfully for a moment and then answered, I believe I will be fifteen in eleven months and twenty-nine days.

I couldn't remember whether you were born or not when your mother's health began to fail.

May I be excused?

Did I say you could be excused?

Five minutes later, his father continued, Would you like to know which of my secrets lasted the longest?

Another five minutes. I know, Chris said.

Are you sure?

Yes. You probably hate the person who told Mother.

Wrong. I hate the person who caused your mother pain. You see a field full of strawberries and start picking. When you get bitten by a snake, should you hate the snake? No. If I were you, I'd hate the strawberries.

May I please go to sleep?

Don't worry, you won't be able to. You'll be up all night trying to figure out how you're going to deal with going without your horse. How you're going to deal with me. Someone will take you to school. Aside from that, you will not set one foot off these grounds. I could send for you at any time. How does that sound?

It sounds like prison.

Doesn't sound like it, my boy, it is.

Chris eyed his father for some time and then asked, Is there no alternative?

There is. You could go to London. Have you not noticed your English? Everyone else no doubt has: You speak just like an Asiatic.

Chris's head jerked up and he looked at his father.

If English like that came from the mouth of a yellow woman, I'd say how adorable, how amusing. The father's gaze frankly assessed his son. You want to tell me how talkative I am tonight, don't you?

Yes.

You don't like my hinting around like this.

No.

Fine. You will stop seeing that goddamned Chinese whore immediately.

I can try.

No matter. Should you fail, you can go to London.

YOU SEEM SURPRISED. Yes, it's been a while since we've seen each other. Ever since you were quarantined at the mission, I've felt it was better not to bother you too much. That building is a memorial hall now, in memory of Dorothy and Mary, the missionaries who rescued you and all the other Chinese prostitutes. I even met the last woman to be rescued. She's seventy-nine, living in a tiny apartment, shabby but clean, her refrigerator virtually empty. She was wearing an old dress she bought at the Salvation Army. She got really excited when we talked about the great rescue campaign. She reminded me of women revolutionaries, who have only their ideals to keep them company in their old age. Her only source of pride in life was having been saved herself and having saved others. She couldn't resist talking about you. She heard about you from the older generation of mission sisters. Because we both knew you, I agreed to go back and see her again.

She was probably so happy to see me because hardly anybody ever asked her about the mission anymore. We talked about how Chinese people don't remember very well what it was like when they first came to Gold Mountain. White people remember even less. Because remembering would embarrass everyone. In 1870 a San Francisco newspaper published the results of a survey in which whites were asked to compare—perfectly objectively—people of color. Fifty percent believed Chinese were worse than blacks, thirty percent that Chinese and blacks were equally bad, and twenty percent that the Chinese weren't as bad as blacks. We also talked about Jack London. I asked if she knew what this author, worshipped by so many young people in China, thought about the Chinese. She said she didn't. I told her I didn't remember his exact words, but I'd never forget the gist. He thought Chinese people were treacherous, lazy, impossible to understand or get close to, and would be of no benefit whatsoever to America. And then I laughed and said, He was my favorite writer as a child, because he had such an impartial understanding of wolves.

Afterward I went to the square near the bay. For seventy years, it's been a gathering place for old Chinese men, a place to play chess, sing opera, and exchange stories about prostitutes. There were men who had gone to sea and when they could go to sea no more, they came here. There were those who had worked their whole lives as ranch hands and then slipped away when they could work no more. None of them had ever scraped up enough money to marry. Yet no matter how poor they were, they'd never be drifters or beggars. For over a hundred years, from your day to mine, Chinese people have rarely let poverty reduce them to begging. Poverty may drive some of them insane, but the madness is always respectable. Those who don't go crazy eat one meal a day, maintaining their dignity in the face of starvation. Jack London never could have imagined it.

Those old men knew about you too. Your story began its travels in this square.

You're famous now. You look more radiant than usual in the late afternoon light, because your day is just starting. There is so much satisfaction in your eyes; you want for nothing. You became famous overnight. I turned to the books and my interviews to see if I could find the real reason for your fame.

Some said it was Da Yong. Some said it was Chris. Others said it was because of the fight on this square.

If you could see all these books on my shelves, of course you'd be embarrassed. How could you know all the ways people lived and died for you? And what could you do about it anyway?

Some of the buildings around this square are coming down, others going up. How could you know that Blacksmith Cai amassed vast real estate holdings by making the weapons for the fight? Night after night, the clanging of hammers on steel went on till dawn, until even the prostitutes blew out their candles to sleep.

You never imagined that those blades would ever have anything to do with you.

You just go on about your business, as beautiful as ever, smiling over things no one knows but you.

The men who fought over you had no idea you had been rescued by the mission and were living in a room so sterile not even a spider could survive there. No one even remembered that you were the cause of the battle, that you had raised the same hope in two different men at the same time, though not on purpose. No one remembered the source of their hatred. Hatred doesn't need a cause.

Look, they are armed with hatchets and cleavers. Most important, they are armed with hatred. They headed for the square. They'd already arranged for the aftermath. If a warrior failed to return from battle, his elders in China would receive compensation from his close friends and blood brothers.

They entered the square slowly, their steps heavy. Each had taken great pains with his grooming, to shave his head as smooth as an egg, to slick his queue with scented oil. They all wore ivory silk mandarin jackets and pants, the better to show any blood. They left their jackets unbuttoned; the long, closely spaced rows of cloth buttons and loops were like teeth. The silk caught the wind like sails, and the deep flapping sounds were stirring indeed.

When bills for the fight were plastered all over Chinatown, the white newspapers published ads of their own, for a huge Oriental gladiator fight. The square was the perfect place for a fight; the balconies of the buildings around it offered excellent box seats. A week before the fight, foreigners were going door to door, asking, Is your balcony for rent? I'll pay five bucks an hour.

Five bucks? Are you kidding me? This is a chance to see Chinese heads with queues lopped off! Five bucks?

You know, the last balcony went for twenty.

The audience arrived by noon. The balconies were set up with shade umbrellas, armchairs, and tables for drinks. Lorgnettes in hand, all the ladies were dressed in their holiday best. Even the buggies that had traveled great distances were decked out for the festivities.

By two o'clock the square was packed. Mexican snack vendors were tunneling through the crowd and the Chinese too had set up booths offering fortune telling, congee, scribe services, and wart removal. Several old men were renting out benches from the opera house for people to stand on.

When the warriors appeared in twos and threes, the crowd cut them a wide berth, reverently holding whatever they were eating or speaking in their mouths as they watched them stride impressively into the square. These were the men called *buhao* boys.

You had seen some of them before. They all had battle experience and the scars to prove it. They had done their share of kidnapping and terrorism, but otherwise they were decent men. They liked to see themselves as coldly detached killers, for to them killing was an art form, and they drew a sharp distinction between themselves and the type who killed whenever they felt like it.

So far, no one has given a thought to the cause of the fight. No one has asked, What about that whore? You've been saved, not just with no quarrel with the world, but separated from it entirely. If they knew where you were, no doubt it would occur to one of them to ask, What the fuck are we fighting for anyway?

The men of each group had black or yellow bands tied around their right arms. Their hatchets and cleavers were decorated with paired tassels like stage props, green and black for one side, and blue and yellow for the other, to match the colors of the armbands.

When everyone was ready, someone came out with fighting words. These were rather tame, maybe an insult about the alleged shortcomings of someone's mother. Any sort of taunt was fair game, useful for getting a rise out of one of the enemy and helping the fighters pair off.

The first pair crossed swords at last. Neither their weapons nor the ways they were used had seen much improvement since ancient times.

By the time more than twenty pairs of fighters had taken the square, all the foreigners could see were flashes of white dancing in the sunlight. They felt like they had ringside seats at an ancient Oriental battlefield. They cheered every deft move. For twenty dollars, they could go sightseeing in antiquity.

The blood on white silk was truly a beautiful sight to behold. Aside from those who had fallen early and been dragged off by an outstretched hand from the crowd, everyone was gushing blood.

The hands of the foreign women were shaking so hard they could no longer adjust their lorgnettes. The men were drinking nonstop, the alcohol instantly converted to sweat, bathing faces that started out red and ended up white. The hairs on the arms gripping the balcony railings were standing on end, trembling like sagebrush before a thunderstorm.

As fewer and fewer fighters remained on the square, the arena seemed to expand. Their shouts were hoarse now and they staggered with every move. A severed hand lay on the ground, its palm offered up to the sky.

Not many remained on the balconies. This little encounter with the Chinese had left them depressed. Someone whispered the death count. Someone laughed coldly and said, Too bad we didn't get to see a head with a queue rolling across the ground. But the laughter was clearly forced.

You knew nothing of any of this. You were being handed from one doctor to another, who openly debated whether or not you would live as you lay there with your eyes closed. You were just one step away from dying.

Death is like anything else; it takes on a lot of different meanings. The same can be said of survival. For over a hundred years now, the notion of survival has held special significance for people like us. You survived in your day and we go on surviving in mine. When we walk off the plane, past the mean, critical faces of Customs and Immigration, we are as bewildered as you were. Just like you did, we feel that the ocean at our backs is nowhere nearly as unfathomable as the dry land right in front of us, and so every yellow stranger we see seems like a next-door neighbor.

We flock to Chinatown too to limit our culture shock. We too crowd into cramped, shabby apartments, a group of us splitting the rent, a sense of safety a matter of everyone feeling equally unsafe, a sense of good luck a matter of everyone feeling equally unlucky. And then, just like your more immediate successors, we begin, step by cautious step, to break out into non-Chinese territory.

As early as the twenties and thirties, the non-Chinese were reaping the benefits in the form of Chinese employees. The young man who was the first from Chinatown to become a manager at a foreign bank in the 1920s changed our history forever.

We haven't changed much. We still quietly toil away, like the Chinese panning for gold in the most depleted mines, using the most primitive methods to accumulate wealth. Our wealth builds up the way dust does, barely. Your industriousness and forbearance have come right down to us, this fifth wave of yellow immigrants.

What about the first woman in the forties to land a bit part in a foreigners' ballet troupe?

Or the astronaut in the sixties?

Just as quietly, we follow in their wake. Chinese in the thirties and forties timidly got on the elevator, walked down the hall, knocked on the door, and submitted their outstanding school transcripts to ask for a lowly job. We're different now. When we show up in our only Western suit, looking people in the eye, spouting good English, and get the job, we take in the towering sky-scrapers and big streets and think, So fucking what? A cynical sneer begins in our eyes and takes over our whole disposition: So this is the position fifth-wave immigrants are fighting for? So what? We're still isolated, as isolated as the first Chinese to set foot on American soil.

Moreover, we don't share the zeal of the gold rush nowadays. We lack our ancestors' faith in gold. Even though you had nothing, you were confident, and we no longer share that irrepressible confidence. In our inexpli-cable depression, our response to the attainment of any goal is: So what? This does not prevent us from trying to make money, but the passionate determination to survive is gone.

We all know how to make this cynical laugh (you, though, are incapable of it) at our own industriousness, at the laziness of foreigners; we laugh at our own evasiveness and the hypocrisy of foreigners; we laugh at our own frugality and at the "we just can't get by" attitude of foreigners. We laugh at the textbook hopes and industry of each wave of Chinese immigrants starting with you, those who succeeded and those who failed.

We are no longer as goal-oriented or self-directed as our predecessors. We cannot even find direction in fighting discrimination. It comes concealed in too many different forms now; it is too subtle, too sophisticated. It is almost like an illusion, there one minute, gone the next, not like in your day, when it came in the form of thugs chasing and beating us up and people like Da Yong had no trouble finding and taking them down.

We don't know who to fight anymore. We have no outlet for our hatred and rage. We have no concrete enemy. The white faces around us all smile in the same typical way, a far cry from chasing and beating. So we don't know what to do.

What other recourse is there but cynicism?

You are looking at my sneer, at my skeptical smile. You don't recognize it at all. You wouldn't even call it a smile. No one would ever have smiled like this in the early or middle periods of our history in America.

But this is not my story. I've already written far too many stories about myself. I just want to look for my roots, in stories about working and studying and getting along with non-Chinese, stories about whether the moon over a foreign land is rounder than the moon back home.

The blood has faded from the battlefield. Listen, some busybody reporter is asking, Who was the whore behind it all?

WHEN THE EAST BAY–BOUND ferry docked, Da Yong and his men got on.

Fusang was wearing a foreign-style hat, its net veil covering her face all the way to her jawline. This hid her cuts and bruises. She had changed her clothes and fixed her hair in the carriage on the way. As someone removed her chains, Da Yong had said, At least that sterile smell of yours is gone.

The ferry had two classes, first class reserved for whites.

When Da Yong sat down, the other men followed suit, but their eyes stayed on Fusang's veiled lips.

She wasn't the only one sitting beside Da Yong. There was also a dog, a parrot, and his jewelry case. He kept looking over these pets of his. When he noticed the men sneaking glances at Fusang's body, he sighed with satisfaction. She was everyone's pet.

Before the boat left, fifteen or sixteen whites got on, saying the first-class cabin was too cold and they'd just have to make do with second class.

All you Chinamen go sit over there! said a man in his forties.

The men with queues looked to Da Yong.

Da Yong took measure of the whites with a grin. They were discharged soldiers, some of whom had worked at sea. These were fellows who took any opportunity to use the Chinese for sport. Each had at least three Chinese punches coming to him.

Da Yong said, I'm counting.

Which meant, We're way outnumbered here.

So the middle of the cabin emptied out, Chinamen on one side, white devils on the other.

Each group spoke its own language and each considered itself lucky to have caught the other in such a good mood.

Each group held on to its own good mood, which also maintained the peace and quiet in the center of the cabin.

But they were also sizing up each other's weaponry and manpower. The white devils noticed Da Yong's daggers right away, first visible, now concealed, under his unbuttoned jacket. They had heard the stories about this Chinaman and his daggers.

Da Yong knew a fight was not in his best interest. He had just broken Fusang out of the mission and the white papers and police were furious that they had nothing to pin on him. In the unlikely event that the police exercised diligence, they might turn up old scores from some of his more recent previous lives. Each time he went under and resurfaced, his calculations grew more thorough. He had constructed such a good temper for himself: Should the tip of his queue get cut off by white devils, he would do nothing more than set fire to one of their stables to let off a little steam. Today, of all days, he had to be on his best behavior, because a huge auction of horses and women, held only once a year, was about to start across the bay, and he had no desire to lose his discerning eye in a fistfight.

Someone muttered, What, has the boat died? Why the fuck aren't we moving?

Stroking the back of Fusang's hand, Da Yong said to the man sitting next to him, Go ask the captain whether he has any intention of making this coffin run.

He had just reached the middle of the cabin when a white man pulled the whiskey bottle from his mouth and said, Get back.

I'm just going to ask why the boat's not moving. . . .

But before the words were out of his mouth, several others roared, Get back!

Tugging on his own queue, bowing slightly at the waist, he said, I'm sorry, I didn't mean to cross the line.

Get back! A dozen white devils raised their hairy fists. Whiskey had turned some of their faces a purplish red and some a gray-green.

The man on his way to find the captain turned and gave Da Yong a hangdog smile.

Da Yong, however, seemed not to have noticed as he kept stroking Fusang, in the same overly intimate way he stroked the parrot's neck feathers.

When the boat started to move, the good mood on both sides returned.

The men on one side of the cabin kept erupting with raucous laughter, while those on the other belted out Cantonese opera tunes as if they had the place to themselves.

Someone pulled out a *huqin* and started sawing away.

Fusang was looking out the window at the water.

Da Yong said, The first time I saw you was three years ago.

Someone was tapping his foot to the beat.

Da Yong continued, This coffin is barely moving. I still remember that river back home, he said to himself.

Fusang's eyelashes fluttered, indicating she had heard him. This moved him, for he liked the fact that she understood what he said, her expression more or less the same as his dog's under similar circumstances.

A boat would come down that river once a month, heading out to sea. He was still talking to himself, as his hand moved from the bird's feathers to toy with a lock of Fusang's hair.

Give me a nice smile now and I'll sell you. Otherwise, I'll have to keep you for myself.

Fusang half turned to him, half smiled to herself.

Da Yong liked the way she made him feel.

Where are you from? Da Yong asked. He never asked about the whores' backgrounds, because the tales they told with those tearful faces put him to sleep. Your people rice farmers?

No, tea, Fusang said.

Whereabouts?

Hunan.

Da Yong's fingers twitched so hard he yanked the lock of hair from her head. A friend of mine, same age as me, has a wife back home, a girl from a tea grower's family in Hunan, Da Yong said. Anyone who knew him well would be astonished to hear him talking like this: Is he all right? He just said something serious!

Fusang said, Oh. Her whole face was turned to him, the sunlit water at her back. She didn't say, Go on, I'm listening. This pleased Da Yong. He felt that with her blank, accepting face looking at you, you couldn't not keep talking.

That friend of mine says he'll go back and see her when he gets a chance, but he can't right now. . . .

With a slight nod of her head, Fusang showed that she understood the friend. She didn't ask why he couldn't go back.

So you were happily growing tea in Hunan. What made you come here?

I was kidnapped.

Who kidnapped you?

Fusang smiled, the way adults smile at children who ask such impossible questions. She turned away, leaving Da Yong her profile, still smiling.

Were you kidnapped from Guangdong?

Yes.

Da Yong took her by the chin and wrenched her face

toward him, his expression darkening. He held her like that for two or three minutes before flinging her chin away. How could this whore have more or less the same background as his own wife? He stared angrily at his hands spread braced on his knees. They looked like starfish clinging to a reef. He didn't want the two women to overlap in any way. His wife was still there, embroidering, pushing the millstone, waiting for him. Each time he sent money home he got the same short, explicit reply from his mother: We got the money, everyone's fine. This was proof his wife was waiting for him. No matter how narrow his escapes from death, when the time came, there would always be a place to take him in. There, nothing he did would be judged and his slate would be wiped clean with a single stroke. There, in his wife's arms. This was why he was so fearless; no matter how bad things got, he always had an escape route, he always had a home to go back to. The reason he sent money home was to maintain this way out. This escape route was absolutely indispensable, for without it, there would be no turning back from all his dangerous journeys and he would be reduced to a life of hopeless wandering. Without that wife waiting for him back home, he might as well whirl the rest of his life away on the merry-go-round of brothels. And so when Fusang's background ended up coinciding so closely with his wife's, he nearly dislocated her jaw. He felt the whore now winning his affection was about to cut off his escape route.

The men singing opera tunes were clearly trying to pick

a fight with those shouting and laughing across the cabin, as more and more of them adopted coquettish falsettos that sounded like the whinnying of horses.

Some of the whites had taken off their shirts to show their scars or tattoos. Surprisingly, they had no objection to the whinnying and just kept on shouting and laughing, their only desire to avoid losing this battle over which side could be louder and more offensive.

Da Yong laughed quietly and said, I've heard farts sound better.

From one to the next, this remark made the rounds. When the singing suddenly stopped, the whites were startled by the crackling silence into a sudden silence of their own and they all looked over, trying to figure out what was so suspicious and threatening.

The thread of the mood in the cabin was stretched to the snapping point.

The boat was just reaching the middle of the bay.

The silence turned from bewildered to hostile, as muscles tightened, ready to strike, eyes already locked in battle.

At this point Da Yong yawned, long and loud. When everyone turned to look at him, he was pulling a bamboo flute from somebody's belt. He inspected one end, then the other, and handed it to Fusang and said, Let's see how it sounds.

Not looking at anyone, Fusang smiled, bent her head, and stuck the flute beneath her veil. With a slight wave of her body, she played a perfectly rounded note.

Da Yong said, Play "Shepherd Su Wu."

Fusang started to play.

The tune was like a gut, winding through everyone there. Everyone's body swayed like Fusang's, even the ones brimming with whiskey.

All fists loosened, like hands submerged in flowing water, letting the current work its way through now limp fingers.

The first time through the song, the whites all had the same fishlike expression on their faces: pursed lips and sad eyes.

The second time through, some of them started jerking as if trying to shake off a spell. They started to realize they were being tricked. What was behind this strange and soulful tune? The Chinamen were using it to gain the upper hand, because the sound was matchless; nothing could drown it out.

The tune played over and over, so monotonously and mysteriously, pouring in through the top of the head, and winding its way all the way down.

All the Chinese were swayed like charmed snakes by the music.

The whites sensed the Chinese were winning.

Stop! one of them shouted, banging a whiskey bottle against a cabin window.

Fusang didn't even hear him. She wound the tune around to the beginning again.

Stop! Stop! Hey you Chinese whore! All the whites were shouting now.

Fusang had just reached a part reminiscent of beautiful sunny skies, of green meadows and red flowers—of course she was in no mood to stop. She looked through her veil at the white faces and then right through them, to a place much farther away.

To the whites, the music felt more and more like torture. The pain was unbearable. This tune showed far too much knowledge of human frailty. It went straight for people's weaknesses and sore spots.

Someone hurled a whiskey bottle to the floor in the middle of the cabin.

Fusang was playing a long descending glide. She watched the glass splashing.

Stop! For God's sake, stop, the man who threw the bottle wailed.

Da Yong stood up and said, Why? Now the Chinese aren't allowed to play Chinese music?

You call that music? You Chinese sons of whore bitches! You call that music?

Da Yong said, What would you call it? Pray tell, you son of a blonde whore bitch, if this isn't music, what is it?

It's torture to the ears of civilized men!

The whites kept shouting for her to stop as Fusang played her way down streams crossing the land like a net, and over scattered clouds in a deep sky.

Da Yong was thinking how truly rare her serenity was. He said to the whites, If you don't like our music, go back to your own cabin.

This *is* our cabin. This is our country, and you can just go back where you came from and listen all you want to this ear-wrecking, nerve-wracking shit!

Stop it! Stop!

If you don't make her stop we'll strip you and throw you all overboard!

The men near the middle were all watching Da Yong, to see if he was going to wind his queue on top of his head. But Da Yong just sat there with his legs crossed, lazily swinging his foot.

Fusang was at an allegro of geese flying south. Her eyes like miles of calm waters, she watched the hostile white and indignant yellow faces. She seemed not to understand why these two gangs were moving closer and closer together.

Da Yong's queue was suddenly already coiled on top of his head.

As Fusang played on, she watched the tangle of arms and legs. Gradually the floor became covered with drops, then pools, of blood. Shoes. Teeth. Hair.

When one of the whites pulled out a flintlock, Da Yong already had his hand on a dagger at his waist. The white man suddenly remembered the legends involving a Chinese thug and his daggers. He wasn't about to test their veracity. He dropped his aim and turned back.

By the time Da Yong had stripped the pants off the last white and tossed him into the water, Fusang had finished the song. Only when she had sealed the last note, and then her lips, did she notice that the men were covered with blood. Every last white was gone.

Sounding its horn, the boat pulled into the dock. Da Yong gathered up his parrot, dog, jewelry case, and Fusang and walked toward the cabin door. Suddenly, he went back, bent over, and started looking for something on the floor.

Someone said, Let's go. The cops are coming!

Someone else shouted, You've got all four, what're you looking for?

Da Yong said, Damn, my finger. He showed them his hand.

They said, They're all there . . .

He said, Dammit, how did I lose a ring?

LET ME TELL YOU what's happened to Chris.

He is lying on his bed fuming over his imprisonment. This is the seventh night of it and he's drinking brandy he bought at exorbitant cost from the cook and running a high fever of rage and longing. At the very same moment, you are lifting your long skirt and climbing a carpeted staircase. This is your new cage, a house Da Yong bought, right between Chinatown and North Beach. You stop on the landing and look back, as if you have lost something. This is the first time you've sensed someone longing for you. You realize that Chris's shadow has been present in these moments when you look back. Take a look at yourself: missing a step, your face a struggle of emotion, like a mute's. You gradually recognize your own longing. You've taken me by surprise here, for longing isn't any part of the you that I know.

Now Chris is leaning against a haystack, both hands behind his head. The sparse blades in the field are tipped in red. He is watching the sun sink into the sea, as gulls flap toward him. He is saying something softly to himself. He's afraid of growing rusty at conversation with you, of forgetting without even noticing the simple language you share.

While Chris is lying in the field, you are pouring water over your body with a brass ladle. You suddenly slow up and your hand trembles. As the water trickles down your body, in rivulets with plans that change abruptly at every curve, you know your longing is back.

While Chris is listening to an Italian farmhand playing a violin, you are putting on earrings. Although you are looking at different things, your eyes meet.

While Chris is looking up at the ceiling memorizing his lessons, you are playing a little game. You close your eyes and when you open them again, there is sure to be something new on the window ledge. A sparrow, moonlight, a poplar leaf. This is when your longing is most intense. You pretend the moonlight, the sparrow, the leaf are Chris as you and they stare wordlessly at each other.

Now Chris is walking into some woods; there is no path. He is realizing how big his father's prison is, that without a horse escape is impossible. He pulls off a leaf and holds it to his lips to make bird calls, the chirping of insects. At that very same moment, you are trying out a new hairstyle. As you look in the mirror, your breath catches in your throat. This is your one hundredth day without that boy, Chris.

Just when everything on his grounds has exhausted Chris's interest, you have finally mastered that complicated coiffure. Now he wanders over to his uncle's study, where his forty-year-old uncle and a group of his father's friends are talking. They are discussing the candidates' attitudes toward China—whose opposition is the staunchest, who can come up with the most expedient plan to get rid of the Chinese, who can most quickly translate the hatred for Chinamen into a political force, and thus, who will get the most votes. Anti-Chinese sentiment is a badge of patriotism for these politicians.

Chris is leaning in the doorway with his hands in his pockets, pursing his lips as if he might walk away whistling any minute. The men in the room don't invite him in, so he invites himself. He walks in and picks up a newspaper from the floor. There is a caricature of four Chinese men with queues, followed by an editorial about how disgusting and inferior the Chinese race is. Before Chris finishes reading it, he suddenly hears a flute playing in the distance. Everyone notices there is something wrong with the boy, the way his eyes have glazed over. He remains in this state until his uncle grabs him by the shoulders and shakes him several times. Chris hears the laughter in the room and forces himself to join in.

While Chris is sitting in his uncle's study, listening to all the bad things they are saying about the Chinese, you are lifting the kettle from the brazier. With a slight tilt of your chin, you pour tea into a cup. A customer is sitting across from you, but you aren't doing these things for him. You're doing them for the pale blue eyes that aren't here, the rapt eyes of that boy. As you pour the tea, the fine hair on your nape stirs and this is how you know the boy's eyes are looking on from some unknowable place.

The customer sitting across from you is Da Yong. Perhaps it isn't strictly appropriate to call him a customer, for he is the owner of the place. He is the secret owner of a great many questionable things around here. His ring-bedecked fingers control many strings, at the end of which are all sorts of illegal goods, like girls or liquor or maybe even a whore like you who commands such a distinguished price.

Maybe the dramatic increase in your price can be explained by your rescue by the mission. Or maybe after the fight, when people saw the men who had risked their lives and died so brutally, they remembered that it all started with you. Or maybe your price had this hidden tendency to soar all along, as early as when people noticed the unusual obsession that cocky little white devil had with you. All the gossip about your relationship made the Chinese and even the whites start paying attention to you. Another reason was Da Yong. He'd managed to drive your price sky high. He was simply too good a salesman. A far cry indeed from salesmen nowadays, who show up at my door and stand there for ten minutes on end, fidgety yet slick, taking what start out as perfectly fine cosmetics, dish soaps, new breakfast cereals, or religions and pitching them straight into the ground, ultimately ruining even my appetite for showing goodwill. Da Yong was the only Chinese in this country who didn't depend on cheap prices to win people over. He knew there is no real value to anything, that value depends entirely upon consensus. Of course, this never kept him from cheating and swindling at every opportunity.

Long lines started forming at your door two months ago. Half the men were foreigners. Whites and Chinese got along better here than ever before, because now they had something in common: you. Two doormen stood in front of this redbrick house with the black roof, each holding a brass basin. Before they went in, each man in line tossed a coin into one of the basins. Then one after another they climbed the stairs, walked into your parlor, and sat alone with you for a while, enjoying your smile, your lips, your teeth cracking melon seeds, the complexity of your hairstyle. Some quietly bent down pretending to pick up their cigar butt and touched the tip of your foot, no bigger than a flower bud. The braver clasped your hand with its painted nails and brought it under their noses for a closer look. You let them. They left after ten minutes through another door. They left in reverie over your scent and smile, feeling as if you had made them a promise. Your sincerity gave each of them an intimacy with you no one else could share. They felt the money was well worth it, for it seemed to them their next date with you was already set, pledged by your smile.

The rich ones would set a time for a full-service appointment.

The latter half of your night was reserved for Da Yong. Whether he showed up or not, you always washed and changed for him and put out fresh candles and tea.

Da Yong loved you the way he loved his dog and horse. The expression on his face when he gave you this necklace was exactly the same as when he fit his horse with an expensive brand of saddle. He would hold your naked body on his lap and stroke you from head to toe, as if you were a giant precious parrot.

You never thanked him for anything. This pleased him, too—his dog and horse and bird never said anything, yet he knew his love for them never went unappreciated. All the pretty words in the world could never be as expressive or true as the nonverbal gratitude of animals.

With all the warmth of a hardened criminal, Da Yong watches you pouring the tea. His smile is laced with the usual lewdness. What a rare pet to smile and pour tea like this!

He can't help reaching out and touching you with his hand, its rudeness gleaming like the diamonds adorning it.

In the moment Da Yong reaches out his hand toward you, you abruptly lift your head. A comet is shooting across the night sky in the window.

At exactly the same moment, Chris is standing at the balcony rail when something makes him look up. The same comet is whizzing across the same sky.

He thinks he has forgotten you. It has been six months.

Six months is a long time in this town. It's a start for some people, the end for others. In six months, a building can go up or come down and be swept away without a trace; the rich can turn poor and the poor can get rich. In six months, trends and even certain streets can change direction. Especially where all the immigrants dumped in this port are concerned, six months is a whole new lifetime. By the half-year mark, I'd learned to stop feeling anything for the families who hired me as a maid; I realized they didn't care about me at all and I just did whatever I had to to survive. By six months, I knew the way to all the cheap markets and secondhand stores and all the routes on which I would not get mugged, on which I could go on surviving. It took just six months to reduce my pride and self-restraint to nothing, to develop in their place a brazen smile, to say to my professors, Aren't I the most qualified for this scholarship? Aren't my grades great? Don't you think I'm working like a dog? My roots, in their painful, itchy attempts to rework themselves into American soil, have learned to twist and squirm, to cling to this place, never to be pulled up.

After six months, Chris, not yet fifteen, rebelled. He took all his money and everything he considered his own personal property and set out walking on the post road to San Francisco.

Let me see what you are up to now. You have gone downstairs and called for a carriage. You're going out. All of a sudden you can't remember whether you were going to Half Immortal Woo's to pick up some medicinal tung oil (for birth control) or to Tailor Mei's to have some clothes made. You tell the driver, Head north.

To the north lies a big variety meats shop and beyond that, a little tea house. The sun warms the tips of your feet just outside the curtain. You have no idea that you and Chris are heading right toward each other, just ten miles apart.

CHRIS WALKED INTO CHINATOWN at high noon.

It was a fine day, sunny and clear, the fishing boats and islands in the bay visible no matter how small or far away. The sun was so bright it turned the shadows of all the houses and trees pitch black.

Chris inhaled deeply, smelling once more the fragrance of incense and opium. He walked right past the shop selling bamboo snakes and other five-cent toys, the gloom inside still as thick as mold. But he didn't go in this time. Six months was enough for him to recognize those things for what they were. He suddenly realized how far he was now from his days of storybooks and toys.

Chinatown hadn't changed at all in six months. The buildings were just lower and more cramped than he remembered, which left him more disgusted and less curious.

A large crowd was gathered outside a shop. People were packed like bricks in a fortress.

Chris was about to walk away when he saw the wall of people loosen to reveal the spectacle that had formed it in the first place. The people on the streets during the day were completely different from those who came out at night. Day people had simple faces that showed their belief that they did honest work. Their faces didn't show emotion easily. Day people had nothing to do with night people. This was a crowd of day people. Because their workday started so early, they were sound asleep by the time night began and had no idea what went on then. Now they were crowding around a woman of the night. They whispered loudly in one another's ears. What a strange sight she was, walking down the steps, straightening her skirt.

There were many white faces in the crowd too. One of them, taking advantage of his height, was glancing back and forth between the woman and his little notebook, where he jotted down the style and fabric of her skirt and the total number of buttons on her clothes.

The woman went into a teahouse but then was trapped there by the crowd.

The tall white man took the opportunity to note that her blouse was embroidered in five different colors.

Someone said, She's smiling, she's smiling!

Someone else said, She's blushing.

She's sitting down, she's sitting down, she's sitting on the threshold!

She's starting to say something, her lips are moving.

She's smiling again.

What's she saying?

She said, Please, I beg you, let me through.

The teahouse waiter had managed to shout a carriage through the crowd. People made just enough room for it to leave.

As the carriage went by, Chris caught a glimpse of her face in the window.

AT TWO O'CLOCK IN THE AFTERNOON, the men lined up outside Fusang's house started to stir. They were busy pinching out their cigarettes, cracking their knuckles, and putting on their hats. They stamped their feet to shake the dust from their shoes.

The line shifted forward.

An artist was selling his supply of color portraits to the crowd.

A doorman, one leg propped on a chair, was chanting instructions to the men, Cooperate with us here, gentlemen; no counterfeit please! If you don't have enough money, just say so, gentlemen, and Miss Fusang will be happy to give you a shorter visit, a little less conversation. May I remind you, gentlemen, Miss Fusang doesn't live on fresh air and salt water—she depends entirely upon your patronage! Don't give us fake money and, on behalf of Miss Fusang, we thank you! As you gentlemen can see, we're shorthanded here, working like dogs; our eyes aren't sharp enough to spot the fakes, gentlemen, we count on your cooperation. You! Beat it. He pushed a man out of line, picked out the coin he had just tossed into the basin, and hurled it away.

How could it be fake?

Beat it.

How could it be fake! You pulled a fast one on me!

Did I say it was fake? You're the one who said it was fake.

The other doorman came over, a range of knives lining his belt like a butcher shop wall. The man finally gave up, picked up his coin from the ground, and disappeared.

Another man near the front of the line told the doorman he didn't have enough money but he did have a sack of dried prawns.

The doorman scooped out a handful, took one look, and said, If you had abalone, I'd let you in.

But we've been shrimpers in my family for generations!

The doorman said, Then I suggest you change jobs.

Standing nearby and trying to make sense of all this, Chris was kicking an empty coconut shell back and forth across the ground. He didn't want anybody to mistake him for part of that line. From the doorman's speech and the banter of the men in line, he could tell times had changed for Fusang, but he still didn't know what to make of it all.

He kicked the coconut like a ball, studying his chances. At the side of the house, he noticed a wall around the yard, topped with broken glass like a row of jagged teeth. There was no hope of getting in that way.

He kicked the coconut around the wall and saw the men who had gone in not so long ago coming out a narrow door, one after another. He heard a man saying, Thank you, please come again.

There were no trees near the wall, just garbage piled at its foot as if washed in by the tide, layer upon filthy layer.

Unable either to climb a tree or to use his mirror, Chris felt the sort of anxiety that only happens in bizarre dreams. In fact, the whole situation belonged in a dream— this luxurious house, all the men it took in and spit out, the pile of garbage. And the inaccessible Fusang.

Chris thought, What has it all come to, in just six months?

A young white guy who had just come out the back door glanced at Chris. He wasn't much older, seventeen or eighteen at most. He looked drunk. His hair was matted with dirt; his filthy shirt was covered with stains and his leather boots with dust. One could tell at a glance by his swagger that he had no idea where he was going next.

Chris wanted to go over and ask him, What's it like in there?

He shuddered. In this total wreck of a man, he suddenly saw himself, two or three years down the road. He still felt like he was in the middle of a bizarre dream. He followed the guy, who was just a shell of a man, drained of all soul by opium, by gambling, by whoring, by the whole filthy, lawless place. A few years ago, he was just like Chris, seduced by all the temptations here, and he had given himself over to them, bit by bit.

Chris saw in the shell of a man he was following the last trace of all those hundreds upon thousands of boys who came to Chinatown in search of playthings.

Chris clenched his teeth at the thought of becoming this guy. He wanted this bizarre dream to end. He had to shake off the pull of this man.

The guy stopped and tripped him and Chris fell to the litter-strewn ground.

Chris glared at him, but he just grinned as he watched Chris wipe the blood from the palms of his hands.

Thinking about it later, Chris couldn't figure out for the life of him why he'd followed the guy into the opium dens, gambling houses, and saloons, lending him all his money so he could turn around and buy Chris so many drinks he got drunk. When the guy suggested pawning the chain around Chris's neck, the one his mother gave him, Chris didn't object. He was no longer capable of objecting.

In the middle of the night, the guy dragged Chris out to the street, checked one last time to make sure he had no more money to lend him, said, See you, and set off swaggering for his next unknown destination.

He didn't even bother to tell Chris what to expect after a drinking binge. Chris discovered that he sounded completely different when he vomited; he didn't know whose voice this was, making the sounds erupting from his mouth. He didn't want it, but there was nothing he could do about it; husky and hoarse, it came spewing out right along with everything else. Just before daybreak Chris discovered that his voice had finally returned to normal. It was as if he had taken some shortcut, to have such a deep, expansive voice for a night.

Back in the middle of the night, though, he was scuttling to the curb every five minutes to find a secluded spot to puke. Before long he stopped being embarrassed and just opened his throat and vomited anywhere. After all, he wasn't the only one. No one complained; they just stayed out of his way.

This place was completely different at night. The gambling hall bosses and female entertainers ran out into the streets, shouting greetings to passersby as if they'd known them all their lives. The minimal standards of decency of the town in the daytime disappeared. Under the cover of night, everybody knew everybody else; everyone was so friendly, too friendly. Chris was constantly being pulled to a stop by hookers, who called him Chaw-lee or Lee-chaw and scolded him for staying away so long.

At daybreak Chris came to a Chinese-style house of red brick with a roof of black tile. Exhausted, he stood looking at the house for a long time. He felt purged after all that puking. He walked up and knocked softly at the door. He fell asleep waiting for it to open.

THE DOOR OPENED at ten o'clock in the morning.

A man came out, barely looking at (or not even seeing) the white boy sprawled across the doorway, stepped over his soiled body (as if stepping over any ordinary obstacle), and walked off. The tapping of his walking stick did not disturb Chris's sleep at all.

At eleven, the proprietor of a laundry came to the door with cleaned and starched shirts, skirts, tablecloths, bed curtains, sheets, and five rolls of foot binding.

The doorman woke up and let the laundryman in.

The laundryman counted out his things, then counted up his money, got up with his empty baskets and carrying pole, and said, That guy out there—how'd he die?

The doorman said, Don't ask me.

Go and see.

Why bother? He didn't die in here.

The laundryman took a couple of steps, then turned

to find the doorman on his way back to bed and said, It's a little white devil.

What?

The dead guy. I think you'd better move him, for appearances' sake.

After I've had more sleep. Seeing the laundryman wasn't going to let the matter drop, he raised his voice and said, If you don't get out of here soon, you're going to run into the cops.

It's much better now; they aren't going after guys with carrying poles so much anymore.

I saw some guys with oysters getting arrested just the other day!

They just happened to run into a mean cop. Didn't you hear? The bill didn't pass—the law against using carrying poles and wearing queues, it didn't pass. As he walked out the door he thought he might as well help out and drag the little white devil off to the side, but then decided not to bother—if they don't care how it looks, why should I?

A little after noon, Fusang decided to go out for some hair oil, since the streets would be empty at this hour. When she opened the door, she retracted her first step in midair. Then she kneeled down and tilted her head to line it up with the face on the ground.

The doorman took one look and said, Damn, I didn't realize he died right in the doorway. He snuck a glance at Fusang and saw she wasn't going to punish him for that remark. He said, I'll go get somebody to toss him somewhere else.

Fusang stood up and said, Toss him in my room.

Huh?

She'd already gone inside and was climbing the stairs when she sensed the doorman's doubts and reconsidered, Okay, then toss him in the bathroom.

The bathroom was filled with alcohol fumes in no time.

Oblivious to the doorman standing there waiting for further instructions, Fusang focused all her attention on the filthy boy on the floor. He slept without making a sound.

For over an hour, she watched him sleep. When he finally moved, she didn't even blink. He just turned over and went back to sleep. He adjusted his shoulders several times without finding a comfortable position, so she wedged her feet into the crook of his neck.

Even as she supported herself on both hands and shifted to lean against the bathtub to make her feet a better cushion for his head and neck, she still kept looking at him, hardly blinking at all. She could see how much he'd gone through. His boots curled, looking more exhausted than their owner. She could tell he'd walked a long time, a whole day and half the night. She could tell the route he had taken: the post road between the ocean and the desert. She could even tell that he'd kept turning down rides. She could see him shaking his head and saying, No, thanks, when a carriage stopped and offered him a lift.

She gently pulled off his boots. And then his socks. He still had the delicate feet of a boy, even if they were as big as a man's. The blisters were broken and bloody.

She took off his jacket, the same navy blue one with the shiny brass buttons. She could tell what he had been doing all night. She carefully unbuttoned his shirt and noticed his necklace was missing. By this point, she was holding him in her arms.

Once he was in the bath, she sat on the edge of the tub and washed off the vomit.

He woke up.

She smiled and said something without really knowing what.

He replied without really knowing what he was saying.

He looked dazed, staring at the body in the water. He didn't seem to recognize it. His mind and body were still disconnected. While he waited to reconnect with himself, he shut his eyes and entrusted his body to her hands.

She brushed the hair off her face and swiped away her tears.

She didn't know she had this in her, to cry like this, her nose so stuffed up she couldn't breathe.

When he opened his eyes again, she was smiling.

He said something.

She replied.

He blushed.

She was wearing the same peach-pink blouse, a long black skirt, and long, dangling earrings. Her English hadn't improved and he still had to rely on intuition to understand her.

She heard the kettle boiling and went out. She realized she was about to have another good cry. This whole business of crying was new to her. She saw in the mirror how different crying made her look, how red her nose was. She thought about how he had worn out his boots and feet over her, lost his necklace and all his money over her, gone completely downhill over her. The boy had finally made it all the way down the hill to manhood.

This was what she had been waiting for all along.

She saw him approaching in the mirror. He came out of the bathroom completely naked.

Knowing he was approaching, she walked over to the kettle, which had been boiling the whole time.

All the west windows were hung with white awnings and the light through them lent a white cast to everything in the room. Including his body.

The tea pouring from the spout of the pot was too dark, like dried blood.

He watched her without making a sound. He held his breath as she brought the cup to her lips to blow on the tea and then flicked her tongue over its surface.

She found there was no distance between them now. The look in his pale blue eyes was white hot. His body and mind had reconnected.

He said something without really knowing what.

She smiled, blushing like a chime, and replied with she didn't know what.

She began to remove her hairpins. Then her earrings, bracelets, and ring. She tossed them on the nightstand.

She didn't know what she said.

He didn't know what he replied. Beads of sweat formed on his lips and the tip of his nose.

There was no need to teach him, she thought.

He swallowed a mouthful of warm spit, watching her.

She drew him into her arms and onto the bed.

She didn't know what she said.

It terrified him. And then he began to tremble.

He didn't know what he said either.

Her breathing quickened. Her skirt slipped with the form and formlessness of water to the floor.

He propped his arms at her sides and leaned his whole body forward. It was as if the force that wanted to rush forward was counteracted by the force that pulled back. His limbs were so long and lean, his brow broader, his cheeks showing adult definition.

But he didn't move.

She opened herself to him.

But he just watched her, his whole body trembling, just inches away from her.

Finally, his lips nestled on hers. Like the lips of a baby nestling toward the milk.

Fusang wrapped her arms around him and pulled him to her naked chest.

Don't avoid me. I know your face is deathly pale.

You are avoiding his touch.

Something very strange has happened: You knew the very first touch of this white boy was trouble.

I thought that was just what you'd been waiting for.

The trouble was a physical sensitivity you'd never felt before. It was as if all your skin had been stripped away, exposing your nerves to light and air. Stop staring at me. I have no explanation for any of this.

As he looked at you, his pale blue eyes were like two holes in a thick layer of ice. His youthfulness gave off a certain muttony scent; the down on his chest became a film of haze in the sunlight. He was so young, yet beneath his faintly freckled skin, he seethed.

Isn't this what you had been waiting for?

You turn to me with so many questions in your eyes, but where do I turn?

All right, you've convinced me to try to explain your feelings. Let me get a cup of coffee first, to find just the right words.

Of course, if I get it wrong, I can always start over.

It wasn't what you'd imagined. . . .

No? Let's try again.

It was the sensitivity. His touch made you ache. Your usual detachment receded like a tide and pain washed in. You'd never known anything like it. You didn't realize it was the price you'd have to pay for commitment and irrevocable belonging. It was almost unbearable. You were no longer free.

You looked at his narrow, flawless body, still not completely grown, the face he had just started to shave.

You became a morass of raw emotion from which your body could no longer shield you.

This is what civilized people call love.

This is what people like me laugh about.

This is the biggest lie on earth.

Don't back away from it. I'm telling you, this is a lie worth dying for, living for, and fighting a whole lifetime for.

I'll tell you this too, Love is what made it so unbearable.

But what do I know? I'm dancing away here and I probably don't know a thing. How can I possibly analyze or explain a historical figure like you? I can't even analyze or explain my contemporaries, let alone myself.

So you just go on about your business. Don't mind me.

WHEN THEY HEARD THE NOISE, Chris raised himself up on both arms and looked at her with alarm.

Fusang brushed a lock of hair from her face. They lay there in silence, craning their necks, the way small animals do when they sniff danger.

When he ducked back into the bathroom, she draped a robe over her shoulders, hastily put up her hair, and scooped a few melon seeds from the plate. When she looked up, Da Yong was already standing in the doorway. She bit into a seed with an audible crack and the blood red shell that came out was broken to bits.

Da Yong stood there taking her in, one shoulder drooping with fatigue and vague curiosity. Then the usual playful lewdness returned to his face. He offered a desultory explanation for his sudden arrival. But really, he could show up anytime with no explanation whatsoever. He was wearing white socks—he'd left his shoes at the front door to be polished. The rule since he bought the place was that everyone getting full service had to leave his shoes at the door and the shoes would be polished and waiting there for him when he left. This kept anyone who might steal something or beat someone up from getting away.

Fusang spit out another smashed shell as she watched him enter the room.

Grinning, Da Yong planted a foot on her dressing table, blocking her in.

Fusang asked him if he wanted her to wash and braid his hair as usual.

Da Yong waited for her to spit out the next shell. He didn't say a thing, just followed her every movement with his eyes, grinning. She smiled, picked up another seed, put it in her mouth, and with a flick of the tip of her tongue gently moved it between her side teeth. The crack was so loud he blinked. When she spit out the shell, it was smashed to bits just like the others.

Da Yong laughed. He knew it: something big was going on, something strange, something that robbed her of her calm and disrupted the rhythm of her breathing for her to be crushing her shells to bits like this.

Who wants to elope with you? he asked with a smile.

She concentrated on extracting the meat of the seed with her tongue.

He's still in this room. Which wardrobe did you hide him in? Never mind, I'll just get my ax and chop him up right along with the furniture. He laughed.

She said, Let me get some water and wash your hair.

Don't take my head someplace else to wash it, okay?

He pinched her cheek.

Fusang raised her head to look up at him with her undivided attention and split open another seed with a crack. This time the shell emerged perfectly intact, its halves still connected like a mussel shell just scooped clean.

He wound his queue around her neck and then unwound it again, looking at her. Something was weighing on him. He wasn't jealous. Others were free to entertain themselves with his dog or parrot, as long as he got them back. A horse that everyone wants to ride is a valuable horse; a real gem shines no matter who wears it and the more times it is sold, the higher its price. Jewels, his horse, his dog, Fusang—what were any of these really worth? He didn't care if thousands of people fondled his treasures, for they were still his, after all. The more people fondled them, the more valuable they were.

But he couldn't flick the weight from his mind. He'd never seen Fusang crush melon seeds like that. There was a big complication somewhere. When he smiled at Fusang again, he was thinking, All right, so we've got a big complication.

He walked over to the chair, plucked his pantlegs at the knees, and sat down as if renouncing the weight on his mind and his whole person right along with it. He closed his eyes and rocked back and forth. He took off his rings, necklace, pocket watch, bracelet, and the gold clips from his pantlegs and lined them up like soldiers on the dressing table behind him. This is what he did when he wanted to rest for a while. Anyone who had designs on him would be momentarily distracted by the battalion of jewelry. Da Yong could use that moment of distraction to turn guard into attack. Most of the time he didn't even have to. With one hand on a dagger at his waist and the other waving behind his head, he'd say, Go on, take them, before I turn around and inconvenience us all.

He let out one yawn after another and several sneezes, all of which he'd suppressed when he was too busy. Then he plucked a strand of his hair, which Fusang had already unbraided, and flossed vigorously, the hair squeaking as it dislodged things that had been stuck there for days. He liked to flaunt everything, including his teeth and hair.

Fusang spread a hot towel over his face. The afternoon sun was too bright and he pulled the towel up over his eyes. His hair fell over the back of the chair and poured like tar into the white enamel basin on the floor. Another smaller enamel basin to the side was heaped with eight eggs. Fusang took one, cracked it, and let the white dribble over his hair.

His hair was famous all over town; let down, it was a piece of black satin, braided, a dark python. The hair that grew on his neck and down his upper back was darker and more gruesome than the hair on his head, like vines in the heart of the jungle.

She knelt on the floor to rub the egg white through his hair. She was listening to the silence in the bathroom ten feet away. Da Yong always fell asleep at this time, but not today. She sensed his eyeballs swinging like pendulums beneath his eyelids. And his cheekbones flexing, as he chewed over some plan.

From the silence in the bathroom she thought she could hear Chris's eyes turning too, his teeth clenched so tightly they ached. She didn't know what had possessed her to hide the boy. Or how she knew that the boy and the man did not belong under the same roof.

Da Yong suddenly parted his fleshy lips, as if straining to listen. After a moment he said, Lovely. Which meant he was pleased with her efforts.

Fusang said, Not a single hair fell out.

Da Yong bellowed, They better not!

She caught a glimpse of something white out of the corner of her eye. She quietly turned her head and there was Chris, bare chested. He wasn't looking at her, but at Da Yong's neck stretched out on the back of the chair. His gaze was steady, the muscles heaving on his boyish chest.

Da Yong's neck was like a tree trunk, toughened by all

sorts of scars. Its prominent Adam's apple bobbed as Chris shifted his eyes to the straight razor lying in the wooden toilet kit. The blade was wonderfully sharp; pushed home into this neck, it would be even more wonderful. The handle was hanging over the edge of the box; it would be so easy to grab.

Fusang saw the plans circulating through his adolescent body. He just needed to take half a step farther. Actually, he didn't even need that, his arms were so long and limber. All he had to do was shift his weight. With the carpet absorbing his fear and excitement, that last step wouldn't make a sound.

He spread his feet and planted them. A ray of the setting sun spotlit Da Yong's Adam's apple. The sun cast a different light onto the razor. The blade was as thin as a sheet of ice already melted through in spots. The neck was stretched out just right; the slice of the blade would be quick and clean.

Fusang saw in Chris's eyes the glint of light on the blade. His lips were so tight they were drained of all color. When she poured a dipper of water on Da Yong's hair, it hung heavier over the back of the chair, stretching his neck even farther. What a magnificent head; it would roll off the chair as the blood was spurting toward the ceiling.

The ending would be like this: Fusang, you're free. You can go wherever you want. You don't have to belong to me; I'm just some guy named Chris. You don't have to belong to the mission or anybody. You belong to yourself.

You don't have to kneel and wash this hair as dark as terror itself. You can walk right out the door and if the doormen try to stop you, you can just smile at them and say, The devil with you. When those men with their real or fake coins come buzzing and swarming around you like hornets, you can say the same thing to them, The devil with you.

And then you leave. Go far, far away. I don't know where, but I'll find you. Maybe many girls will leave with you and then find themselves living to twenty, to thirty, to forty. You'll know where to go. Maybe you'll leave the city, the state, along with everyone else who hates slavery. More and more people are leaving all the time, you know, because they don't want their children growing up around slaves; they believe the buying and selling of human beings is evil. They're all leaving, leaving behind slave girls like you, leaving to build an all-white society. Maybe you'd better not go with them, after all. But the world's a big place. All I know is you're free. You should find a place to spend your freedom.

Chris felt himself of gigantic stature, if not a giant. But this was no fairy tale. He was a real, live knight, brave and true. The feet that had held the same stance all this time were now as steady as steel in the stirrups, as he looked down at his beloved slave girl below, You're free.

Instead, at this point, someone said, Hey, you can go now. Before I turn around.

It took Chris a long time to register Da Yong's insolent voice. A sleepy contentment rumbled in his throat and was muffled by the towel.

Chris was jolted from knighthood back to his ordinary self. He didn't know what to do.

Da Yong said, Go on, get out of here. I hear your daddy calling you.

The razor glinted. Chris began to reach for it.

Fusang did nothing to either encourage or stop him. She just knelt there, combing the black hair from top to bottom, over and over again.

Chris didn't like to admit it, but it was a beautiful sight. The beauty came from harmony. Kneeling made her alarmingly beautiful.

The water from Da Yong's hair dripped into the basin. Fusang wrapped the hair around her hand to wring it out.

Chris sensed the sunlight on the blade go out. His urge to grab it was also fading. In light of Fusang's composure, it seemed senseless, absurd. Thoughts of rescue, of setting her free, just clashed with the beauty around her.

Now Da Yong said, You're still here? Don't you get it? Yellow women have the same parts as white women. Those tabloids of yours are just stupid when they claim that after the white women's bodies you're used to, you might go in the wrong door with a yellow woman. You didn't take the wrong door, did you, my boy?

He chuckled as he whipped the towel from his face

and turned his chair to face Chris and Fusang. He looked like he wanted to go on discussing this with Chris.

Fusang shifted her weight onto one leg and turned to the side to move out of the way. Da Yong grabbed her by the loop of hair she'd hastily put up over one ear earlier. His eyes had trouble adjusting to the darkness after the direct sunlight and he couldn't help squinting as he looked at Chris. His dripping hair soaked the carpet like rain.

Chris wished he'd grabbed the razor when he'd had the chance; Da Yong had it now.

Holding Fusang with one hand and the razor with the other, Da Yong smiled at Chris and said, You want her?

Chris didn't know which answer would spare Fusang. He was preparing to lunge at any moment.

Let her go, Chris said. I'd like to see you go straight to hell.

Who wouldn't? said Da Yong.

Do you want to buy her out? Da Yong asked a few moments later.

Yes.

Okay. Da Yong nodded. I've always known you're not like the other little white devils who come here looking for cheap thrills. What'll you do with her? Take her to church and get married?

Why not?

My, my. Don't you know it's illegal for whites to marry Asians or blacks?

We can go to another state.

Huh. Da Yong studied the razor, Fusang, and what Chris had said. Still smiling, he loosened his grip on Fusang's hair and checked the sharpness of the blade with his thumb, his expression and the motions of his thumb equally obscene. Looking at Chris, he handed the razor to Fusang.

He said, See? She handles a razor every day. He turned to Fusang, You know how to use a blade, right? You don't need this little assassin, do you? Here, show him.

Da Yong lay back in the chair and said, Her technique is marvelous.

Clenching his fists, Chris watched the rise and fall of the razor as Da Yong shifted and twisted his mouth and neck to accommodate it. The blade evenly scraped his face, jaw, and neck.

He asked, Is it sharp?

Fusang said, Yes.

It better be!

The razor in Fusang's hand was steadily rounding the Adam's apple on the enormous neck.

Chris watched the blade as it passed one perfect entry point after another. Again and again his hopes sank. Suddenly, Fusang lifted the razor and turned to him, as if she was about to hand it to him. But she just wiped the blade on the towel beside her cosmetics case. She smoothed her hair, as if she had only just remembered he was still there, and cast him a warm look, as if everyone in the room belonged to the same household.

Da Yong was breathing loudly and deeply. He'd fallen asleep. The last light of the sun shone on a tooth stranded outside his lips.

Chris was exhausted.

That harmony was back again. He couldn't understand it, this harmony of cruelty, evil, danger, and a glinting blade. Even he had no desire to disrupt it. For now he was part of it too.

Without knowing how he got there, Chris was already downstairs. Just as he was about to go out the door, it occurred to him that the bizarre dream that had begun the night before had never ended—it had been going on the whole time. It included the doormen now eating noodles, impossible tangles pulled into their mouths. And it included the world beyond this door, the gambling halls and opium dens and whorehouses, all the haunting images.

ONE DAY MANY YEARS LATER, around the time he was forty, Chris remembered how he felt when he left Fusang and Da Yong's house that day. Everything came back to him, even details he hadn't remembered before. Fusang was kneeling, dressed in soft silk that traced the shape of her body. He couldn't remember what color it was, but sometimes he imagined it was the color of her skin. She might as well have been naked. He just remembered it was a beautiful image. Because deep down she really was free; she had the kind of freedom that rescue or salvation could never bring, the kind that nobody could ever give or take away.

But Chris hadn't understood that as a teenager. He hadn't understood that even he was a threat to her freedom.

It upset him that he hadn't understood. He was filled with remorse, shaking his head, now gray at the temples. He remembered how he had felt when he walked out that door. His distress had turned to hatred. He hated the Chinese quarter. He hated these people. He watched their little yellow bodies bustling in the twilight. You could never tell whether they really liked or hated one another; they all seemed to have a deeper understanding of one another, deep to the point of collusion. It nearly drove him crazy.

As he walked down the street that day, he looked at everything in despair, hating everything he saw. His moral compass still had only two poles: right and wrong; it was useless now, and he was lost without it. He'd wanted to smash this refusal to make proper distinctions between things. He'd wanted to smash those hideous Oriental buildings, all those grotesque feet and queues. He'd wanted to smash everything he couldn't understand.

Chris at middle age shuddered with the realization that the destruction he had longed for included Fusang too.

Had he really hated the woman he'd loved his whole life? Chris looked into the depths of his heart. The answer was yes.

AT FIRST, NO ONE PANICKED at the sight of the flames; there was always a fire somewhere or other in the city. Most of the houses had been thrown up in haste, with no planning for fire. Nothing much lasted very long in this place, where everyone just rushed in, grabbed riches, and then rushed out again. After a robbery or murder, people set fires to destroy the evidence of their crime.

The audience was sitting in the theater as usual, watching an opera. The screaming outside was drowned out by the screeching onstage. Several foreigners had taken seats on the crude plank benches, to see the beautiful young woman who was really played by a boy. They came often and the more they watched, the less they could believe she was a boy. As the fire raged outside, she was just taking the stage, her two bleached, seemingly boneless fingers performing the orchid gesture in a grand sweep from beneath her sleeve, her tiny waist twisting ever so slightly, to much whistling and applause below, and a voice far rougher than hers wailing, My little darling!

The fire burned halfway down the street before anyone took it seriously.

Chris was on his way home when he too was stopped in his tracks by the sight of the flames.

People were chasing and attacking one another, and horrendous screaming filled the air. Chris asked a white man what all the fighting was about.

He hurled a broken whiskey bottle at a produce shop and said, Where are you from, the moon? It started a long time ago! Some Chinamen stripped the pants off some bastards and threw them overboard! That was a few months ago. The police never caught them. Then today, a few hundred sons of bitches have this big meeting at a warehouse and by night there are thousands of them! They're thinking, How come I got fired? Of course it's the Chinamen!

In the firelight Chris suddenly recognized the man as the one who had borrowed all his money and left him drunk on the curb the night before.

Two Chinese women came running up and without even waiting for Chris to duck out of the way, started yelling at the guy and hitting him on the head with their tiny shoes. Though he wasn't hurt, the novelty of their thrashing style left him momentarily uncertain over how to ward them off.

Chris crossed the street aimlessly. Everyone was aimless at this point.

There was a crowd of whites, wearing armbands with a slogan some politician had come up with: Chinamen Must Go! They were shouting about destroying the Chinese quarter so Chinamen would have nowhere to hide opium and slave girls anymore. They charged all the way through Chinatown without realizing it and then came charging back, raising dust like a stampede of raging bulls.

Chris was swept up in the tide, no longer acting on his own. The anger of the crowd was contagious. Along with everyone around him, he began raising his fist to the night sky roiling with smoke. At first he was ashamed of the slogan he was chanting, but ten minutes later he shared the righteous anger of the crowd.

A forty-year-old white man with black hair was giving a speech from a Chinese sedan chair carried by four brawny, neckless Spaniards. The brocade curtains were open and his thick beard was long and straggly.

The opera had stopped a long time ago. Another speaker was onstage now, ticking off on his fingers the crimes of the Chinamen—gambling, opium, the selling of children, the owning of slaves. These whorehouses and gambling halls and opium dens are what the yellow race has brought upon us all!

And rats! someone shouted from below.

Out behind the theater, the white opera fans were chasing the boy who played the young woman. They were shouting, Hey little darling, hey pretty girl! The little darling had climbed a tree to the rooftop like an alley cat, her long red skirt in tatters, one of her watery sleeves now shorter than the other. When the twelve-year-old boy was finally caught, many mouths sought his cherry red lips and many hands tore off all his clothes to see at last what was really underneath.

The speaker inspired Chris. These people were freeing slaves, freeing all the Chinese slaves sold into this place by their brethren. He realized that on his own, he could never free all the Chinese slave girls, never mind Fusang. He had to join forces with a crowd like this. He imagined himself charging into her house with them, a torch in one hand, a sword in the other, and telling her, You're free. The crowd would smash her cage. He would destroy all her misfortune.

DON'T LOOK OUT THAT WINDOW behind you. Just go on playing your flute.

But what about the mob out there? I want to know what's gotten into them too. Look, it's right here in this book—can you believe it? "It was simply a few men and boys who had lost their jobs vandalizing the Chinese quarter. . . ." I don't think it was so simple. There had to be political motivations involved, a sense of righteousness. The crowd must have felt like the armies of the Crusades. A sense of duty will sanctify the hoodlums in any crowd. This is the only explanation that makes sense. It had to be the will of them all and not just a few who happened to be playing with fire in Chinatown. That's the only way it could have taken on the momentum it did. The account I've got here reads, "Many homes and businesses were burned to the ground and dozens of Chinese prostitutes were dragged into the streets and raped." Could that have happened without the will of them all?

There's arson and murder all over town, which is keeping the men pretty busy. This leaves you plenty of time to play the flute.

It's all far away for now. Seeping through your tightly shut windows, the chanting about Chinamen just sounds like the ocean in bad weather.

I checked many sources for the exact location of your house and found it right on the border of Chinatown. This was a bold choice: Two laundries that had moved to get away from the crowding in central Chinatown were quickly burned to the ground. It's only because this little pavilion-style house of yours set a death-defying foot into non-Chinese territory that the crowd is leaving it alone for now; no one is throwing rocks through your windows to hear the crying and screaming of Chinese whores.

As you play your song "Shepherd Su Wu" with a faraway look in your eyes, your coworkers are being hauled into the streets, their cries for help dying in their throats, their foot bindings pulled off and strewn all over the ground like rotting entrails.

Don't look. They'll be here soon enough anyway. Let me use this time to tell you about a show I just saw on TV.

Wait, do you smell that? It's smoke coming in the window behind you. They broke down the doors of a warehouse a few streets over and dumped out hundreds of sacks of dried oysters. Oysters were all over the place, the greasy stench so vile that hundreds of people all started puking at the same time, the retching erupting from their chests like thunder. Then somebody decided to fight the stench with fire. But that just made it worse. Now people couldn't open their eyes or breathe through their noses, let alone stop the surging of their brains against their skulls.

Someone exclaimed, Chinamen actually eat this crap!

You know, he was really saying this, People who eat this crap will eat anything. People who eat this crap can use anything in the world to strengthen and multiply. People who eat this crap will be mighty hard to wipe out. No wonder these Chinamen are so hard to kill.

The stench just wouldn't go away. Some tried to put out the fires but it wasn't so easy. Oysters were wriggling and squirming all over the ground, each tiny body crackling and screaming.

You see? Anger can turn to hatred just like that.

Hatred is amazing. It makes people self-righteous; it drives them with a sense of mission. I'm not talking about revenge; that's too simple. People are born with a higher form of hatred, so immense it doesn't even need a target. Like love so vast no object is necessary. This kind of hatred can lie dormant for years, like a swell of darkness, and people are never even conscious of it. But once the darkness is breached, all rationality drowns and the things people do out of hatred serve only the purpose of fulfilling an overwhelming emotional need. Burning, smashing, killing, rape—they're all just channels. It doesn't even matter what started it, because people quickly become intoxicated by the sheer spectacle of destruction. Like love at the earth-shattering stage, hatred by this point feeds on itself, simply for its own sake. The pleasure of watching some person or thing destroyed by one's own hand is virtually orgasmic.

When I was a child I saw those sexual impulses they called the cultural revolution and those orgasms they called rebellion. The gratification of hatred produces the same rapture in everyone.

You'd better get away from the window. Yes, close the blind too. Don't pay any attention to the doormen downstairs.

What are they shouting? Duck, hide, run away?

You're right, you never run away.

Stop looking at me that way, as if I know what all those people out there are going to do to you.

I do know. Just as future generations know what I'm going to do next or what others are going to do to me. What those skinheads on TV are going to do to me. We don't know what they're planning. We fifth-wave Chinese abroad are still waiting, just as you are now.

The jackboots are coming this way.

Hundreds of feet are marching up the street, which is strewn with underwear. Riots bring out all the dirty laundry. In San Francisco in 1870, it cost just as much to have your clothes washed as it did to buy them new.

To stay in business, Chinese laundries sent boatloads of dirty clothes back to China to be washed. When the clothes came back three months later, their owners were long gone. Some had left, some had died, and some had changed their names. The clothes wound up in the pawnshops. Most people just shelved the dirty and bought clean. During riots, though, with all the torching and looting, trunks being tossed and wardrobes dumped, all the dirty underwear ended up on the streets, muffling the hoofbeats of the riot police when they finally arrived.

This eyesore took the hatred to new heights. It reminded people that the Chinese quarter was and always would be filthy. As long as they were in a good mood, they accepted the filth as atmosphere, ambience. Or they came up with relatively tame jokes about it, which have made it from your day to mine.

The marchers are downstairs now. You taper off a note and raise your head to look at me. You know that only those of later generations will be able to figure this whole thing out.

The doormen bolted the front door and pressed their backs to it with their eyes closed; their whole bodies shook with the kicking from outside. They'd already set aside their knives, which were useless against foreigners because you'd get the gallows whether you killed anyone or not.

You just keep looking at me, the lingering notes of your flute still winding around my head. With all these history books and interviews, of course I already know what they did to you. But how could you believe me? How can I make you believe this hatred as vast as the sky?

It's just like the hatred of the skinheads on TV, so immense yet totally impersonal.

After I left you yesterday, I turned on the TV and came across a talk show about hate groups. There was a group of people in their twenties, their heads shaven bald, a dark metallic blue. Their faces were pale and grave. There were four or five women in the group, their eyes just as cold as the men's. They all had swastikas tattooed on their arms and legs. When they announced their hatred for Asians, blacks, and anybody else who wasn't white, I was shocked.

You know, if I hadn't been so shocked, I would have called in with a question of my own.

With shock that bordered upon reverence, the audience kept asking, Why?

The skinheads smiled with cold detachment and said they were under no obligation to explain; they weren't looking for anyone's understanding.

Bombarded with questions, one of the men said, You coloreds can live; we're not saying we want you dead; we just don't want you living where we do. We want someplace where we don't have to look at you or put up with you at all. His voice was cold with ruthless finality.

An Asian woman, a student, asked, Why do you feel you have to put up with us?

A young African-American man said, Isn't it really the case that we have been putting up with *you* all these years?

The Asian woman, now plaintive: What have we ever done to make you feel you have to put up with us? Where did this hatred between us get started? It's never been mutual. Never!

His face excessively white, the skinhead said, If we didn't put up with you, we wouldn't be able to control our hatred and that would be worse for you. If we had some land completely separate from you, we wouldn't have to tolerate you anymore.

The student persisted, What've we ever done to you? We've never done anything wrong! Why should you have to tolerate us?

The skinhead: Under present circumstances, we have no choice.

The student: We don't want to be merely tolerated!

The skinhead smiled with haughty exasperation. When the noise in the audience died down, he said gravely, We fully believe that one day we won't have to tolerate you. We have some important work ahead of us.

As if he had planned it that way, he refused to say what it was. The obvious threat made us all extremely uneasy. Leaving us hanging under that threat, he said, It's like this: We just hate you.

Let's see what these hateful people are going to do with you. What that important work turns out to be.

Where are they taking you? Twenty or thirty men are

listening to the ripping of silk all over your body and watching you stumble as if drunk as they push you back and forth.

Someone says, Look at her feet! Chinamen call them sexy!

She's the corruption of all morality and decency!

The street is pitch black, for all the gaslights have been broken.

Now I see it: a horseless carriage.

You have been dragged inside and men take turns coming through the curtain.

You don't call for help; you don't bite or scratch. You reach for the jacket of each man, and during his wild heavings, you bite off a button.

You don't call them names, you just open your body toward an expanse of nothingness. You concentrate on opening yourself, time after time, except for your fists, which are full of buttons.

When the police finally arrive, your hands are full of buttons of all shapes and sizes.

By daybreak the fire is out. You gather your buttons and take them back to your house, which has been torn apart. You put them in an empty powder box, put on the lid, and shake it back and forth, listening. I've never seen such a strange expression in your eyes.

Chinatown revived first thing in the morning, lest it lose a single day of business. It had already reconciled itself without much thought to what had happened. But the look in your eyes reminds me of the cacophony of the insane who cannot speak.

From then on, you'd take out the box whenever you were alone and shake it next to your ear. As if you were shaking someone who refused to answer you.

How can I explain it to you, this terrible thing called rape?

The rapists returned to their respectable lives. When they discovered a button missing, they were just as puzzled as you.

IN THE DARKNESS, Chris found himself part of a crowd.

Someone was yelling, Tear her apart!

What were they up to? Chris saw a guy stripping off his belt.

What're you doing?

You'll see soon enough!

Let me go!

You little shit!

Beat him up! The little shit wants a fucking too!

Take your hands off me! Let me go!

You yellow whore lover!

The men had important work to do; their rage was terrifying. All Chris could hear was ragged panting. Finally he realized it was his own.

DA YONG WALKED PAST the burned-out buildings of Chinatown, past a pile of burnt oysters, then foot bindings, embroidered shoes, and colorful silks in tatters.

Two men with disheveled hair were carrying out a big basin of fresh soy milk. The owner of a teahouse was chewing out one of his workers, who retorted with a silent litany of facial expressions. Someone came around the corner to dump slop buckets, three in one hand.

Da Yong said to the teahouse owner, Go make me some tea.

The owner told his worker, Go make some tea.

The worker said, Don't you know? All the teapots got used last night against the *guailo*.

The bamboo works was busiest of all: All the lanterns in the whorehouses had been destroyed and they had to make hundreds to replace them.

Leading his horse, Da Yong looked around. The place was as still as the aftermath of a typhoon. All the debris had been piled up, the first sign of new life. Morning was just starting a bit later than usual.

The night before, when he first saw the blaze, Da Yong had been in the East Bay. The fire was nothing spectacular at that point. One saw fires two days out of three in this city and he had set a few of his own. He went into the auction without giving it much thought.

The girls had already stripped and were lining up to be weighed. Third Uncle was pinching their arms and legs, offering random comments on their bodies.

Da Yong sat down in a chair against the wall and finished his cigar. He no longer chewed tobacco, because it wasn't fashionable. Besides, he could add another article of jewelry to his person with a fancy cigar cutter at his waist. Putting out his cigar, he noticed a girl who seemed a bit bigger and taller than the others and he looked her over.

She was seventeen or eighteen and clearly avoiding him.

Da Yong said, Third Uncle, you gave one of them three catties of water to drink.

Water? Third Uncle retorted, I had to feed them three big bowls of congee each. They didn't get a bite of it for two whole months on the way over.

Da Yong started flossing his teeth. As he shifted his mouth, he kept his eyes on the tall girl. He checked over the spaces between his teeth with his tongue.

Third Uncle said, Such a shame, after that terrible storm, only these twelve left from the whole load. Plus, most of the potatoes rotted, so a good number starved to death too.

Twelve? Da Yong said. I count thirteen.

With an expression of momentary confusion in his eyes, Third Uncle said, Oh? Well, better one more than one less!

Third Uncle waved a cattail leaf fan around the huddled girls to keep the mosquitoes off their bare skin.

Da Yong told him to take the tall girl back to the scales and weigh her again. The girl hung from the steelyard with her eyes closed, biting her lower lip.

Da Yong walked up, checked the weight, and said, I've seen this one before.

Her eyelids flinched.

Da Yong said, See? She understands English.

Her eyelids flinched again.

Da Yong told one of the men holding the steelyard, Go find Gimpy Chan. Make it snappy. Tell him to hurry up and find the red veil from last time and set up the canopy. The last one ran out on him, so I'll buy him a prettier one! This time we'll cripple her first, make one of her legs shorter than the other, just like Gimpy Chan's, so she can't run away.

The guy looked at Da Yong as blankly and earnestly as a dog.

Go on, hurry up, Da Yong said. Just repeat what I said and Gimpy Chan'll know what I'm talking about. Tell him he doesn't need to wash his face, just wipe the crud from his eyes and I'll supply the bride.

Still a little hesitant, the guy started to leave.

Third Uncle grabbed him and said with a nervous laugh to Da Yong, Pay up first, you gotta pay me first.

Da Yong said, I'd pay for the other twelve, sure, but not this thirteenth piece of shit!

Third Uncle said, There were thirteen! My eyes are bad; I just missed one!

Da Yong said, Your eyes are bad, all right. One slips in at Customs and you don't even notice.

Third Uncle had been fanning the girls rather steadily and now he stopped.

The tall girl suddenly wished she were shorter. She

hunched down and hid her face behind her disheveled hair.

Da Yong said with a chuckle, You snuck in to get some congee along with the rest, right?

The girls were as unresponsive as a pile of meat.

Which one of you was it? Da Yong asked.

Nobody made a sound.

So you've already been brainwashed by this spy. Fine. He walked up to the tall girl and bent down to find the face hidden behind her hair.

In her attempts to avoid him she was forced to lift her head.

Da Yong pulled her from the group. Come on, come on, let me get a good look at you, it's been so long. Let's see, the last time I saw you, you were wearing Rescue Society sackcloth, weren't you?

Covering her crotch with both hands, she looked like she was wishing somebody would hurry up and stab or shoot her.

Da Yong said, The Rescue Society made you a spy and snuck you in at Customs to find our secret passageways, right?

Da Yong remembered that he had noticed the fire getting bigger when he was taking the girl to Gimpy Chan's shrimp camp. But he wasn't paying any attention at the time, because he knew the girl was a spy and he had to act fast.

He hadn't expected such large-scale disaster. The theater doors were gone and workers from the gambling houses were scouring the ground for mahjong tiles. More and more people were coming out now and excavating the debris, shouting with delight whenever they found something.

The day before, the Rescue Society missionaries had arrived at Chan's shrimp camp at daybreak. As soon as Da Yong saw the men behind them, he knew they were vigilantes. The missionaries announced to the guests at the dawn wedding banquet, You can't marry our translator.

Gimpy Chan, the forty-year-old groom, came out of the bridal chamber limping with joy. When someone told him what the missionaries said, he replied, How could I be so lucky? My bride's fresh off the boat from China.

He pointed to the mud shack, where a woman covered with a red cloth from her face to her knees was sitting on red bedding.

Take off that veil, we want to see her, Mary said.

Gimpy Chan turned to the guests who had pushed their way to the front, What did she say?

She said take off the veil, she wants to see her.

Gimpy Chan laughed. I can't wait to see her myself.

Dorothy said, If we can't see her, how can we be sure she isn't really our translator?

A guest translated for Gimpy Chan.

Gimpy Chan laughed even louder and said, Believe me, I'd love to find a translator under there! She'd know how to read and write and would be pretty besides!

Dorothy said, How could you marry our translator?

If I weren't crippled I could! I hear they can sing foreign songs—it would be like getting a bride who was almost white!

One of the guests translated this. The white women's faces turned bright red.

Over a hundred wedding guests got up from the mismatched tables and crowded around. When the men saw Da Yong calmly coiling his queue, they followed suit.

Mary noticed and gestured with her eyes to Dorothy and the vigilantes.

Thoroughly sensible, Dorothy said to the crowd, We just want a look at her. We just want to make sure she isn't our translator.

One of the men in the crowd said, What would your translator be doing here? Unless you sent her in as a spy.

Mary said, Watch your mouth. We would never resort to such deplorable measures.

So what measures do you resort to?

One of the vigilantes said, There's no need for all this nonsense. He headed for the mud shack festooned in red, pulling out his gun.

Suddenly, the girl in the bridal chamber got up and headed for the door. Her limp was every bit as pronounced as Gimpy Chan's.

From the back of the crowd, Da Yong admired his handiwork.

The bride leaned in the doorway as if she longed to join the party.

Mary held the vigilante back and reached for the veil, the movement of her hand slowed by the outcome hanging in the balance.

With a sag of her shoulders, the bride sniffled and blew her nose onto the ground.

One of the guests shouted, Don't worry, Gimpy Chan, if they lay a hand on her, we'll peel them like shrimp.

Someone else said, Gimpy Chan lost his first wife and it was no easy task to find him a perfect match this time. Now it turns out she's a translator!

Others said, You can't even keep track of your own translator; what's she doing here?

Spying, that's what!

So let's see her! I've always wondered what a spy girl looks like.

The missionaries talked it over and then said to Gimpy Chan, We'll get to the bottom of this in court.

Da Yong left the shrimp camp right behind the missionaries. He knew it was over and his side had won. Lulled by the sleepy gait of the horses and the wine from the wedding banquet, he smiled to imagine the missionaries coming back to the shrimp camp in four or five months. They would find a bunch of women sitting in a circle, peeling shrimp, their fingers flying. The translator or spy would be long gone, no matter what you called her. Now she would be just another village woman getting a penny a pound for her work, peeling and jabbering away like the others.

Or perhaps the missionaries might see in the distance Gimpy Chan shouldering his poplar pole, carrying shrimp in one basket and a pregnant woman in the other. The woman would be complacently gnawing on a piece of sugarcane. Da Yong nearly laughed aloud imagining the missionaries who'd been so determined to rescue her just standing there watching as the woman was carried down the highway into town, spitting out sugarcane pulp the whole way.

The morning after Gimpy Chan's wedding, Da Yong had come into town when the sun was two feet over the horizon.

He discovered his hands ached from gripping the reins so tightly.

An old man with a basket on his back was picking through the dirty underwear on the ground looking for fabric to paste and sew together into shoe soles. He picked up a red silk lapel and held it up to the sun.

The red silk in the sunlight caught Da Yong's eye. It was better than the rest of the cloth on the ground, each blossom the most expensive embroidery. He recognized it.

The old man said, I'm the one who found it.

Da Yong said, The fuck you did. He snatched it from his hand, throwing the old man to the ground.

When Da Yong ran into Fusang's room, she was eating a milk white fish head. She said, The soup's ready.

He just stood there weak-kneed and then stumbled toward her.

She was wearing a short white wrap. The skin from her open collar all the way up her neck was scratched like a freshly plowed field.

He pulled her into his arms. After a long time he said, I'll have to kill you.

Fusang saw his black eyes glaze with tears. She suddenly noticed that the fish bone in her mouth had been sucked of all flavor, so she spat it into her palm.

He said, The owner of the fabric store across the street killed his wife this morning.

With a slight nod, she looked earnestly into his eyes, which were growing increasingly misty.

They dragged her into the street for a whore, Da Yong said, and he just helped her kill herself.

Fusang said with a faint smile, They were husband and wife.

Da Yong said, If you were my wife I'd help you. Don't worry, I'll give you a decent burial, just the way I would for my own wife. Remembering something, he pulled a jade lock off the chain around his neck. I'll put this in your mouth so your body won't rot.

Fusang knew she'd never get such treatment while alive. She looked at him with gratitude.

As he looked back at her, his pupils were unfathomable.

He lifted her up and laid her on the bed as solemnly as if burying her.

She asked, How many left in your family?

That's not for you to ask.

Oh.

Through a film of tears, Da Yong took in the beauty of her acceptance of death. Like a tamed animal, she faced everything with this same silent complacency. He opened her collar and slowly reached for the knife in his boot. The expression in his eyes and his every movement showed how much he treasured her.

Fusang said, Make sure you get somebody in to do my hair.

Don't worry, I'll see to it you look good.

Da Yong had pulled out his knife. He found himself holding it like someone who had never used one before. He realized he had never killed anyone with a knife, just his fists, his feet, or a butt of his head. A knife would be no fun at all. How many rounds could he go with a knife? Besides, who could possibly be worth killing with a knife? A knife would seem much too serious, much too committed.

Fusang put her hand on his chest, waiting for him to ready himself. Her hand traced down to the five pretty daggers in his belt.

Use one of these, she said.

Don't move.

Da Yong came to another realization: These daggers were nothing but jewelry. He'd never known how to use them. He'd taken them off the corpse of someone he beat to death many years ago. He'd never had the chance to learn to use them, because before he could ever get around to it, his enemy was already pretty much dead. His dagger maneuvers had grown more and more legendary precisely because no one had ever seen him resort to them; word was by the time you saw the dagger, it was already in you and the poison at the tips was a mixture of several different snake venoms. He suspected the Chinese had deliberately spread these lies to the foreigners, claiming they had seen with their own eyes how he delivered those daggers with such miraculous aim and speed that he had but to touch the daggers and you were dead. Over time the matter reached such a degree of efficiency that all he had to do was flash open his jacket and put his hand to a dagger and his adversary would crumble or capitulate. The daggers had gradually become a symbol of his powerful aptitude for battle, his ability to kill without batting an eye.

Fusang said, Don't forget to eat the soup I made.

As he looked at her, what came to mind was the river back home, old and young women lined up on its bank waiting for the postman. Threaded needles stuck through their aprons, they were eating peaches or lichees or plums. One of them was his wife. The knife in his hand drooped, and he said to Fusang regretfully, If you were my wife, I'd kill you.

Fusang had never seen him so serious.

He continued, If I killed you, it would be out of love for you. Do you know that?

Fusang nodded.

Looking away, Da Yong shook his head. I've never loved anyone enough to kill her. There's no woman worth the bother.

He let Fusang go and got up, tossing his knife into the air and catching it again. He could no longer recall what had been racing through his mind when he ran up the stairs. He certainly wanted to kill the white devils who had torn up Fusang, but the one he wanted to kill most was Fusang herself. He'd always believed that a man only killed the woman he loved best.

He found it hard to believe that he really cared about her so much.

A few days before, someone brought him a message from home, saying his wife had come over to find him. This news was several years old, because his mother had forbidden anyone to tell him, for fear he would stop sending money or never come home or exact even more blood debts. Only after his mother had died did anyone dare tell him the truth. His wife had been here looking for him for years; she might be any new woman he met. On any given day, some poor and virtuous fishwife squatting at the market scaling fish might lift her sallow face to him, start rummaging through her apron, pull out a raggedy letter, and say, I've found you at last. His mind felt bloated and sore at the prospect.

When Fusang saw him sheath the knife in his boot, she slowly got up from the bed, her own mind feeling bloated and sore, because she'd never imagined that Da

Yong loved her as if she was his wife. He'd wanted to take her life almost the same way the shop owner had killed his wife. She thought, So I'm not exactly the same as his gems and dog and bird after all.

He had a lot on his mind when he left.

Fusang went back to eating the fish head, watching Da Yong from the window. He walked east for a bit, then suddenly turned and headed south. She noisily sucked the brains from a gap in the bones she had cracked with her teeth, releasing a delicate burst of flavor.

SO WHAT ELSE do you remember?

Yes, it was a very foggy night. You're right. There was no moon. When those men pulled you into the carriage, the fog surged in through the holes in the curtain.

Your memory is correct: You didn't scream at all.

It was a long time ago and they aren't prosecuting anyone involved in the riot. But you still wonder who they were.

Not only did you not scream, you were as amenable as fog. You simply accommodated the pain.

At the time you were thinking that one's allotment of pain in life could tear and converge like fog. Like fog, you enveloped each man stabbing into you. And after a while the pain was no longer so sharp, no longer tore you completely apart.

After a while you couldn't tell the difference between what was suddenly taking place on your body and what took place there every day. You couldn't find any real difference between selling your body and gang rape.

What does it mean, anyway, to sell oneself? People think you sold yourself. But what about all these women around me? Times have changed. Look at all these women setting prices for themselves: a house, a car, an income of so many thousands per year. Okay, it's a deal. They just call it something else: marriage. Wives sell themselves nightly, their bodies mute and aloof as merchandise. In return they get three meals a day and closets and drawers full of clothes and jewelry. And this isn't the only way it's done. Some sell out for power, others for fame. Some sell themselves for a city residence permit in China or a green card in the U.S. Are there any women out there who *aren't* selling themselves?

Aren't I? How many times have I lain unwillingly beneath a man, like a pile of merchandise?

Perhaps the ability to confuse these things is a blessing. Stop looking at me that way, Fusang. I'm not crying.

I don't remember any better than you do how many bodies pressed down upon you. You just enveloped them, one after the next, the way fog envelops rocks no matter how jagged, seas no matter how savage.

You just pulled or bit off their buttons. You did this without any clear goal in mind. It never occurred to you that you would be called in to identify suspects afterward. And of course, you weren't. You collected these dozens of buttons for yourself alone, to remind yourself of this occasion of such peculiar contact with men.

In the gray light before dawn, as the police cavalry came charging in from the distance, you collected your battered self and all the buttons as if you were picking up shells on the beach.

Many days went by before you suddenly remembered the kiss. It was totally out of place. Nothing was different at first, but as he came toward you, there was a pause. And then all his movements slowed. His palms were smooth and ice cold as he brushed the hair from your face.

That was when he kissed you, his lips fastened to yours, without moving, just fastening you there.

You broke away. You didn't know how to deal with those lips—they were a cruel prank, mocking you.

You tried to break away from the man who was kissing you. Being kissed made you recoil. Completely overwhelmed, you suddenly felt something you had never experienced in your life: humiliation.

Your strength drained away and all you could do was rest your arms on his back. His body was different from the others and this bothered you. The others were big and fast, rough, hairy, covered with scars. This one was soft and smooth.

With your last remaining strength you bit a button from his jacket.

AS THE DARKNESS FINALLY BEGAN to thin, someone was pulling a filthy figure from the ground, shaking and shouting at it. With extreme effort Chris realized the one being lifted was himself and the one lifting him was his elder brother.

Chris slept all that day and through the night. When he finally woke up, he noticed a slip of paper on his nightstand. He blinked at it and it slowly dawned on him what it was: a steamer ticket to London. His father had kept his word. He picked up the ticket and held it up to the morning light. He remembered the night his father had spoken of sending him to England as the ultimate punishment. But it didn't feel like punishment at all.

By the time he got up, Chris was almost elated. The cook and the Italian handyman both noticed the change in him: He whistled "Oh Susanna" with an innocence bordering upon idiocy and he ran down to the beach with the other boys in the neighborhood to build sand castles, something he hadn't done for a good four or five years. He even went out of his way to help two of his little girl cousins fly a kite. It was as if he'd become a child again overnight. He stopped brooding like an old man. It was as if everything he'd done between twelve and fifteen had just been a stage performance and now that version of Chris, the one who slept all day when his brother brought him back from Chinatown, was gone. But this new version wasn't right either; it was like a grown-up deciding one day to put on the clothes of his childhood.

Chris happily told everyone he was going to a grammar school in London; he would live with his mother's younger sister and during vacations he would travel all over Europe with his aunt. No one knew why he was so happy to be leaving home.

On the afternoon of his departure, he heard his two girl cousins shouting and laughing in the yard. With all the impulsiveness of a boy, he climbed out the window to join in the fun.

They were jumping up and down watching a kite flying high in the sky. A Chinese kite.

He jumped and shouted too. But as the pink-and-black kite with its wavering tail grew smaller, something started to bother him.

His cousins smiled with a respectful distance at the Chris who had recently not seemed quite himself. They weren't sure why he was being sent to London. He must have been part of some scandal, or done something truly remarkable, to be getting such special treatment.

Chris didn't want to watch the kite disappear. He looked down and smiled at his cousins. The knowing smile everyone in the Koehler clan used with one another, fiercely intimate and utterly alone.

The cousins watched a bit fearfully as he walked off. They didn't know what to make of his joy a moment ago and his sudden bad mood now.

Chris didn't want to see anybody. He wanted to go to the library to get a couple of books, but he was afraid of running into his father or uncle. Successfully avoiding everyone, he took the books from the shelf and some newspapers from the sofa and returned to his bedroom like a shadow that startled no one. This house was amazing—everyone could have his own routes, on which it was possible to avoid interacting with anyone else.

A servant was checking his luggage, reciting aloud from a list. When he finished, he handed the list to Chris, who held it as if in a trance, the servant's words echoing over and over in his mind: Three jackets, one missing a button.

Three jackets, one missing a button. Chris tried not to admit to himself that he knew when he had lost that button and how. He told the maid to pack into his bookbag the newspaper that had come the morning after the Chinatown riot. He told her he was too busy to read it. He would read it on the ship, where he would have plenty of time to kill.

It wasn't until some days later that Chris opened the newspaper. Fusang's picture was right in the middle of a long, detailed article about the rape during the riot. He stared at the picture, at the face he had loved since twelve, and watched as the wind yanked the paper from his hands and blew it into the water. He had to grip the cold railing with both hands to keep from touching the space on his jacket where the button had been. Then he took off the jacket and threw it into the sea.

It was early morning and a band of pale pink above the water was deepening in color. He suddenly turned around to look for something, anything—a younger kid to play a spelling game with or any sort of game into which he could senselessly flee and not have to think.

During the two years he lived in London with his aunt, he kept busy with schoolwork and reading poetry and novels. He even took part in amateur theater and went with his aunt's family to church every Sunday. He didn't often think about his life in America, of which everything had faded, including the woman in red. Once or twice, when he strolled through a grove of blossoming plum trees near his aunt's house, he thought about what might be done with the petals. They could be crushed into a beautiful red juice and used to paint the fingernails of a Chinese woman. The image pained him. He realized that the hurt had never gone away; he'd just refused to feel it. It wasn't that he missed her. He didn't need to. She was a part of his growing up and coming of age.

After he had graduated from English public school with outstanding marks, his father wrote to say he could come home. Standing at the railing of a ship moving in the opposite direction now, bringing him home, he remembered the newspaper and jacket he had buried at sea. Now he was seventeen and could recall without shuddering everything he had done that dark night, from beginning to end.

He'd never let himself think about it at fifteen. He simply couldn't think about the jacket with the missing button. He thought back to the days when he ran around hiding and playing like an idiot, trying with all his might to convince everyone he was still a child. He tried to convince himself too that there are certain things children simply don't do, or even if they do, there is just no comparison with the same thing done by an adult. Nothing a child does is ever a crime; the world makes so many allowances for children. When his brother brought him back from Chinatown, Chris tried to be as childish as possible, to take cover in childhood from a conscience that was already growing up.

Chris now thought to himself, Being a child is so safe. Anything a child does wrong, no matter how terrible, is just a mistake, a prank that went too far. A child has a whole lifetime ahead of him in which to change, plenty of chances for a fresh start. No matter what crimes a child commits, the length of the future ahead of him allows them to just be dismissed as mistakes. A child can do anything and then step back, back into childhood again.

Adults brag about the mistakes of their youth. They'll even admit with indulgent smiles their illicit loves or acts of theft. Even if they continue to do these things as adults, they have only enough courage to cover the selves of their youth.

Chris at seventeen was brave enough to face the crime he had committed two years before.

He thought about it often. About Fusang's unfathomable beauty. Their relationship seemed even more unfathomable now than it had at the time. The more he thought about it, the braver he felt. Like any Koehler, he would never hide from his conscience. The Koehler men believed in guilt and found it deeply satisfying.

Unlike the rest of the men in his family, however, seventeen-year-old Chris thought about trying to make it up to her somehow. He would atone with his everlasting longing. His crime had already cut off all the next steps between them. He would never go see her again.

Over the past two years, he had caught himself time and again whispering in that language of Fusang's. When he used it to form apologies, he seemed to be forgiving himself at the same time. Who could believe there was enough hatred in the world to engulf anyone, to draw anyone into a crowd that was driven solely by its own momentum? Each person became a mindless body, just hands and feet realizing the will of the crowd. None could escape the control the crowd had over him.

Fifteen-year-old Chris hadn't. And so he'd just done what everyone else was doing to her.

He never imagined it would be Fusang.

But somewhere in his mind he had hoped so. If by some chance she remembered the only one in the darkness who showed a little bit of tenderness, he thought this might give her some consolation. Maybe it would help make up for the awfulness.

Chris jerked his head away from these thoughts. He had raped her. He had wanted to take her with force. He was stunned. He had finally found the courage to unbury his most terrible secret. Had he really had no idea whose body that was? He'd tried to understand it through a layer of silk so many times. Because he'd never had the chance to see her completely naked, he knew her body in ways that didn't depend on sight. He knew it better than that. How could he pretend he hadn't recognized her?

By taking things to the point of no return, he would no longer have to endure the torture of his confusion over the real feelings between Fusang and Da Yong, his confusion over Chinese people in general. By taking things to that point, at least he could free himself from all that confusion. Let them go on killing and enslaving one another! He couldn't understand it and he didn't even want to anymore.

Before leaving London, Chris had received a letter from Dorothy. She said the Rescue Society was starting a school for the Chinese. She asked him to take a teaching position, partly for pay, partly as a contribution to the cause. After a few days of indecision, he agreed. It would be good to get some experience before starting college. He also considered it a way to repay Fusang.

And so this is the Chris we have coming to Chinatown now. With a young man's exaggerated sense of his own maturity, a sense of the inevitability of his past mistakes and enthusiasm over the chance to make a fresh start, he walked once more through the narrow, bustling streets. There was just that same inept expression in his eyes.

He devoted himself to his work. Every day he taught four hours of English and then two on the U.S. Constitution and spent the rest of the time studying for his college preparatory classes or going out to play polo with new friends. He got along well with his students. One of the girls, named Amy, a bright fifteen-year-old, wanted to go to nursing school. He liked her and when he discovered she had feet as big and wide and good at running as white girls' feet, he was so relieved he laughed with joy.

Chris wanted to ask Amy out. Soon they were taking a walk together nearly every Sunday afternoon. The body beneath Amy's gray cotton skirt held little interest for him, just enough to keep him going on walks with her.

For months he successfully avoided thinking about Fusang.

THE NEWS THAT FUSANG would be put up for auction ran in all the papers for days.

It was the year after the big Chinatown riot.

She wasn't really being auctioned. Da Yong had decided to marry her off. It didn't matter to whom, as long as she could recognize him by name.

Da Yong had changed since the riot. He would sit on the stoop of some shop, his eyes vacant, picking up a handful of gravel and every now and then tossing a pebble into the street. Anyone he happened to hit would say, Who did that?

From beneath the wide brim of his black hat, Da Yong would say, Who else?

His dress was so conservative now that sometimes it could even be called drab and he didn't wear jewelry anymore. He stopped oiling his queue and it hung scraggily down his back. The soles of his black cotton shoes were no longer white; chips of polish had flaked off around the edges. The word spread like wildfire: Da Yong had lost his mind.

Further proof of this was found in the fact that he was giving away the two youngest of the ten girls he'd just bought. He left the two five-year-olds at a busy intersection and whoever wanted them could have them. But nobody did, for no matter how useful they might be in the future, it would take a lot of time and money to raise them to that point. Besides, Da Yong had announced beforehand, The brothels will not get their clutches on these girls.

Four days later, two people from the Rescue Society showed up and read the placards hanging around the girls' necks, on which the intention to give them away was spelled out in both Chinese and English. The missionaries looked around in every direction before finally deciding to rescue the girls, whether it was a trap or not. They lifted them off their feet and ran off, the girls bawling the whole way.

One day a few weeks later, Da Yong went to Fusang's house. There was a line out front as usual. The doormen said, Here for the receipts?

Da Yong said, What receipts?

The doormen were speechless. He really had lost his mind if he couldn't even remember the money he collected every two weeks like clockwork.

Da Yong suddenly turned to the men in line and said, Go home, all of you. As of tomorrow, Fusang will be yours.

Everyone was shocked.

Da Yong continued, When you come back tomorrow, make sure you've had a good bath and combed all the lice out of your hair. I'll marry her to whoever she can recognize by name.

The men stood there in shock for a moment and then left.

Da Yong told the doormen to close up early; he and Fusang would be parting forever, so they needed more time than usual.

The more they talked it over, the angrier the doormen got: For all their years of loyalty and courage, they wouldn't even have anywhere to eat lunch tomorrow.

Shortly after midnight, when they had split the money Da Yong hadn't bothered to collect, they crept up the dark stairs, one from the front, the other from the back. The sound of their footsteps was submerged in the thick carpet. So were the random creakings of their joints.

The lamp in Fusang's room was out. The long farewell was over and she and Da Yong had gone to sleep. One of the doormen tried the door and it pushed open without a sound. He mapped out in his mind the arrangement of the furniture in the room as he switched his knife to his left hand and wiped the sweat from his right on his pants.

Just as he was putting one foot through the door, the

knife in the process of changing hands, he heard a voice behind him. When he turned his head, he saw Da Yong standing right at the back of his neck.

Da Yong said, Get out of here.

The knife fell to the carpet.

Da Yong had just taken a piss and was holding up his pajama bottoms by the waist.

The doorman knew he would not see daylight.

Da Yong said, Pick it up.

The doorman obediently bent down and picked up the knife and didn't bother to get up. He figured he'd get knocked down again anyway. Then Da Yong ordered him to stand.

Da Yong had left his pajama sash on the bed, so he was still fumbling at his waist with one hand.

He held out the other for the knife.

It had never occurred to the doorman to defy Da Yong. Now the matter was even clearer: Whether he defied him or not, fought back or not, the result would be the same, the only difference being the amount of effort involved. He handed over the knife.

Da Yong took it, tossed it in the air and caught it again, but it didn't feel right in his hand no matter how he held it. He said, Go get what I left in the toilet.

The doorman knew Da Yong was afraid not only of awakening Fusang, but also of messing up the carpet. He thought, It's better to be stabbed in the back anyway—I won't have to go through the terror, or bother to duck.

He knew the other doorman had already run off with the money, so he would have to take the wounds for two. When he got to the toilet, he saw the daggers lying beside the slop bucket. They were sheathed in fine leather, their ivory handles inlaid with white gold, looking very old and very unused. He suddenly realized that in all the time he'd been with Da Yong, he'd never once seen him use them.

The doorman picked up the daggers, this revelation clear in his mind.

Da Yong said, Bring them here.

The doorman had never imagined that his last steps on earth would be taken from a toilet to his own executioner. An executioner who didn't even need a knife.

As Da Yong took the daggers, he handed back the knife and said, You'd better get out of here while you still can. When I wake up, it might be too late.

Mumbling his thanks, the doorman scurried off, afraid Da Yong would change his mind before he could reach the front door.

The next day, Da Yong set Fusang up in the living room. She was covered with a veil embroidered with the red phoenix facing the rising sun and wearing a heavily embroidered wedding dress. Da Yong had hired a dozen or so hatchet men for crowd control and they patrolled the place inside and out, their hands stuck in their jacket pockets.

As instructed, the contestants walked up to Fusang and

greeted her. Each said a few words to describe what had gone on between the two of them in private. Then they held out their hands for her to study, since they all had rings or tattoos that might remind her.

Fusang was sitting up straight in an armchair, one foot in front of the other, the bridal headdress under the veil shaking slightly from time to time. They couldn't see her face, but her posture was smiling.

For three whole months, she didn't get a single name right. There were some who came dozens of times, figuring that if she ran through all the wrong names in her head, she would hit upon their own eventually, but she was wrong each and every time.

Her smiling posture gave each man complete confidence: She's bound to recognize me this time, he thought.

Later, Fusang stopped bothering with names; she just gave a soft, apologetic laugh. The mood of the crowd was always cordial; for rich and poor, handsome and ugly, old and young, yellow, black, and white, this was the first time they had been treated equally.

Many came from other states, having checked the latest notice in the papers each day. These notices didn't occupy much space, but they occupied it regularly; for six months running they came out daily like the stock market report.

After six months, the men started dwindling in number, like gamblers who never win and end up quitting without ever really intending to.

Around the one-year mark, Fusang often found herself sitting alone all day long. It never occurred to people that she was waiting for someone in particular. Her face was hidden beneath the red veil, but she would lift her chin like a village woman standing on a corner, waiting for the child who would show up any minute.

She was sure that one day a hand would be held out before her with no mark or sign of any kind, that even the timidity and recklessness, the smudges and clumsiness common to boys his age—that even those signs would be gone. But she would recognize him anyway.

Now Fusang was no longer waiting. She took up embroidery, macramé, and cooking. When Da Yong came, she'd make an extra dish. She still liked wearing a pink blouse and long dangling earrings. Da Yong would tell her each time he came how many girls he'd given away. He promised Fusang he'd make sure he placed her somewhere respectable.

Every now and then Fusang would go out, holding either a paper parasol from a Japanese shop or a huge silk fan to shield herself from the crowds. The place she went most often was still that teahouse. It had changed owners, been spruced up considerably, and no longer sold the cheaper grades of tea; people like the produce vendors had stopped coming.

The customers it drew now were managers and foremen from factories that made socks or shoes or cigars. Their speech was liberally mixed with English. They would pay for Fusang's longan soup and send the waiter over to ask her the same thing.

How about it? The smoking room in back is nice and quiet.

Fusang would smile and say, Some other time.

In time, the men stopped asking. Those who adored her so much they couldn't stand it enlisted the waiter to press upon her a bouquet of silk flowers or a cake of fine powder; some even gave her gold earrings or a gold ring. They all knew such gifts could never be worthy of her and so when she accepted them, the men's smiles were somewhat ashamed as they watched from across the room.

Fusang knew some of them had wives at home; that they could show her such regard made her smile back at them most gratefully.

One day she received three rings and had just put them on and was looking across the room to acknowledge their senders when two yellow girls and two white boys came in. They all looked like students. Each girl wore her hair in a single long braid, brought around to the front where she could coil the tip around her fingers.

The men at a table of factory managers waved at them.

The girls waved back. It was as if neither had noticed the other was of the opposite sex.

Fusang looked on with great interest. Especially note-worthy were the feet of these two girls, flat and wide as a boy's, wearing black leather shoes on crossed legs swaying with such freedom and ease—Fusang found it most interesting indeed. She knew the Rescue Society had opened a school that had over a hundred Chinese girls for students. But this was the first time she had ever seen these girls with her own eyes.

Fusang followed them to the schoolyard gate. Classes had just ended and girls came pouring out of the building, walking just like boys.

Fusang tilted her face, watching with growing fascination.

When the last of the girls ran out, a blond head appeared. Then his shoulders and chest. The chest under the white shirt and gray vest was broader now. His long, lean legs were pencil straight and he still walked with the loose stride of the horseman who would rather be riding, not graceful but unusually energetic. His boots were covered with dust, just as they had been when he was younger. Even at twelve he'd always looked windblown and travel-worn.

Like a young mother who notices her son has become a man overnight, Fusang felt the blood rushing to her face.

She never thought, Oh, there he is! He never came to see me. He's back at last—where had he gone anyway?

These thoughts never occurred to her. She felt no resentment or blame. She just stood there, her face bright red, looking at him, all grown up.

Chris felt someone looking at him. He went on

chatting with a student as he looked around. But he didn't notice the cluster of pink that was Fusang and returned to his conversation with greater attention.

Finally, he started toward the gate with a group of girls.

There was a second in which Fusang and Chris looked right at each other, but he just returned to his conversation, as if he hadn't even noticed her. He would have to pass right by her to go out the gate. Her heart calm and steady, Fusang turned and faced the wall.

She didn't want those girls to see her.

She also wanted to play a little hide-and-seek with Chris.

Maybe she didn't really know why she turned around, turned her whole back to the gate.

When he was twelve, his first sight of her had been from the back.

Fusang heard his voice and footsteps drawing closer, but they showed no sign of stopping. His voice reached her before his footsteps did. It was right behind her—she would have bumped right into it had she turned around then.

But then his steps grew cautious, hesitant. He stopped right behind her. If she turned around, the distance between them would have collapsed the same way it did in that white room at the Rescue Society.

But the footsteps kept on going, right past her.

When she could no longer hear them, she turned around and saw that all the girls were gone. There was only one left, walking beside Chris. Her feet were huge.

ON THAT AFTERNOON in late May, Chris saw Fusang. She was standing with her back to the schoolyard gate, her hands clasped in front of her. The breeze caught her long black skirt and her earrings swayed like wind chimes.

Chris didn't stop. Maybe he stopped for just a moment before he walked past her. On the occasions afterward, he probably walked straight past her without stopping at all.

After the seventh time or so, Fusang stopped coming. Chris, however, took to lingering a long time at that wall.

He had decided that he could never go see her again; precisely because the nonfeet under that long black skirt made him crave her like an addict, precisely because he knew she was the only woman in the world who could set off such cravings in him, precisely because anticipation was written all over her soft and graceful back, he could never go see her again.

The new Chris ought to have the willpower to suppress those cravings.

How could he go back? Going back would mean making the same mistake all over again, except this time he could no longer take cover in childhood. His childhood had ended in that dark carriage two years before.

Unless of course he bought her out and married her.

Chris would never marry a Chinese prostitute. That had been his whim at fifteen, but he wasn't fifteen anymore. After Fusang, how could he look twice at any of the other Chinese girls, so bony and pure? He could see

· 243 ·

through them at a single glance, and if he'd seen through one, he'd seen through a hundred. There was only one thing he could do with them and that was propose. Their faces would look the same in bed as they did in the classroom. The whole point of their lives was to be offered to someone in marriage. They would marry someone like Chris, who respected the institution of marriage but had no enthusiasm for it whatsoever. Chris couldn't imagine a marriage any different from his father's or uncle's.

Maybe someday Fusang would come to know that among those who had genuinely cared about her and her kind, there was a devoted young teacher named Chris.

Perhaps she would eventually realize that he was staying away from her as a way of coming clean, of punishing himself.

One day when he was waiting for Amy at the Tree of Heaven Teahouse, Fusang walked in. From all the way across the room he could smell the fragrance of her hair, the starch in her clothes, and her body's own indescribable scent. Her skirt swept heavily across the floor. Her whole person had always been so substantial.

She didn't approach his table. She gave him a smile and walked over to a table across the room.

Before long, he heard cracking sounds—Fusang splitting melon seeds with her teeth.

He couldn't help turning to look at her. Her lips and teeth were as expressive as ever. He saw now that she had never used just one method of cracking melon seeds.

Sometimes she put the whole seed in her mouth and chased it around with her tongue and teeth and sometimes she just put it between her front teeth with her fingers and then bit into it lightly, at which point her chin would tuck to her chest and her eyes would deepen. Her loose sleeves swung with the movements of her hands. Around the black satin band at the hems of her powder pink sleeves was a row of flowers embroidered in many different shades of pink. This made her profile even more beautiful.

Not a single word of his conversation with Amy registered. Without bothering to interrupt, he just listened to her talk about everything under the sun in her nearly perfect English. When Amy laughed, he knew he should too.

He quickly noticed that Fusang wasn't paying any attention either to whatever Amy was saying; her attention had wandered off somewhere.

Perhaps it had wandered to the same place Chris's had. To those earliest days, when he was twelve. Fusang was helping his childish hands hold chopsticks. She looked on with an indulgent smile as one chopstick crept past the other and he had to keep stopping to line them up again.

How could he possibly substitute Amy for Fusang? Who could ever take Fusang's place? Sitting there so simply, cracking her melon seeds, drinking her tea . . .

And Chris had thought he could stay away from her.

When Fusang saw him looking back at her from the door, she smiled. The same as always. It was as if she'd never noticed he'd been gone so long.

THEY RETURNED TO THE TEAHOUSE the same time the next day. Chris arrived a moment after she did. The waiter sidled up to him with a knowing look and said, If the gentleman would like a good time, our smoking room in back is free.

Chris blushed.

The waiter said, Just leave me a little tip.

Without waiting for Chris to respond, he'd already hurried over to Fusang and said, I told him.

Fusang nodded and rose from her chair, looking at Chris. Her face was as red as his, her eyes sparkling.

There were three rattan chaises in the smoking room, all of them a bit tattered. Unlike the pitch black walls of opium dens where business was thriving, the yellowed walls here proved that hardly anyone ever came. The whole place looked abandoned, even though the waiter had been through it with a feather duster. Dust motes were still rising, dancing for the two of them in a ray of sunlight through the window.

Chris's senses expanded as if he had been drinking. What swelled through his mind and body crowded out all thought. This was a place for addicts, and until the craving was satisfied, the filth and shabbiness of the room would go unnoticed.

Neither of them said a word.

He had to show he was different. He was a real john now. Determined. He knew what he wanted. No more detours. And no talk. Talk required thought and real johns couldn't afford to think. Real johns didn't mention love or longing, didn't talk about feelings they couldn't express properly anyway.

She looked back and forth at the chairs, trying to find a safe place to sit down. Watching him looking at her, she sank into a chair with ease.

The rattan creaked.

The real john crumbled. As he walked toward her, he realized with wonder and dismay that he could never be a real john with her.

She was removing a garland of fresh orchids from her hair when she saw him approaching and shifted to one side of the chair as if to say, sit here.

He watched her take off her bracelets and necklace. At twelve he had watched her like this.

He put his hand on her arm, to tell her to stop, that he couldn't stand the rush of so many memories.

She said, I don't want to scratch you.

He was suddenly annoyed that he had grown up, that he was now a man who could do anything. He wished he could go back to his younger self, younger than twelve, young enough to nestle into her bosom and take the next natural step and suck at her nipples.

Fusang lifted her hands to fondle his earlobes. Her hair was still up and her face was unusually composed.

He wanted to tell her something. It was because of her

that he had been punished by his father and forced to leave her. But he had never forgotten her. In the London brothels, whether he kept his eyes open or shut them, she was everywhere. When he pleasured himself, it was her name he grit through his teeth. He was sick; she had made it impossible for him to ever find the state of mind in which he could share proper love with a girl. But he didn't say anything.

She had many things she wanted to tell him too. She had waited a whole year for him under that red veil embroidered with the red phoenix facing the rising sun. At the sight of every one of those unfamiliar hands, she was wondering what the hands she knew so well were doing. But she didn't say anything.

She opened the last clasp on her blouse.

Chris grabbed her hand to stop her. He had to explain the real reason he'd been avoiding her. What had led him to start anew, to pay for what he had done. He had to tell her what he'd done to her with those big hairy men on that foggy moonless night. But he couldn't.

Fusang's eyes seemed to be asking, Why don't you treat me the way other johns do?

For seven or eight days running, Chris tortured himself with guilt. Every afternoon at dusk, he and Fusang met in the opium den in the back of the teahouse. She gave and he took. She indulged him and he let himself be indulged. He even followed her wishes and did everything he could to act like a normal john, to act like he wouldn't be getting his money's worth if he didn't expend his every last ounce of energy upon her. Afterward, time after time, he was stunned: You've used her again under false pretenses!

Right up to the day when he disheveled her hair in his passion.

A brass button rolled out.

Chris stopped like a horse reined in at the edge of a cliff.

Fusang slowly turned her face to see him reach out for the button as it rolled across the floor.

Without even waiting for it to stop, he knew where it had come from.

Fusang's eyes followed his hand and the gold shine of the button in it. She had known his secret all along and had been keeping it for him. Chris didn't know whose secret it was anymore.

Who was this woman? A saint who could forgive anything? Or a hunter who set such good traps that he would never escape?

Over the past two years, he had rehearsed so many regrets and apologies and now he couldn't say a word. How could he have imagined this next step? She had turned her goodwill into forgiveness and her forgiveness into a net and, suddenly, escape was impossible. He was a prisoner for life of his own conscience. In that net of forgiveness, she had even taken away his chance to tell her what he had done.

What could he say now?

Tears ran down his face. He didn't care about his dignity anymore. He began sobbing openly.

Fusang's eyes filled with tears, but she didn't let them fall. She was simply keeping him company in his crying. When a mother sees a child sobbing with such pain, she is bound to be affected.

She put her arms around him and pulled his head to her chest. After a time, she slipped to her knees, her arms still around him. She wanted to wipe his tears but he kept pushing her away.

He saw her kneeling form through his tears. It was beautiful.

She knelt there, forgiving the whole world once more.

MANY YEARS LATER, Chris at seventy, up one night with insomnia, saw the image of Fusang kneeling again. She was wearing the same pink blouse, but she was smaller than in his earlier memories. The image moved him like nothing else could. He hadn't forgiven very many people in his life. He had always been so good at finding fault in himself and others and now he realized that his whole upright life had been ushered along by Fusang's forgiveness. On this sleepless night, he found the woman in the pink blouse kneeling in the distant past heartwrenching.

He thought, What made the image of Fusang kneeling so moving was the fact that it embodied the age-old compassion of women for men.

At this thought, he raised himself out of bed. He began pacing the floor, but the bedroom was too small for all his thoughts. He walked out onto the veranda holding a glass of brandy in his trembling hand.

FUSANG HAD BEEN THINKING for many days now about Chris's sobbing and what he'd said afterward, I want to buy your freedom.

Later, when he'd calmed down, he told her he would take her to another state and marry her. When he saw how stunned she was, he said, Forget about our differences.

He also said, On our wedding day, you can give me back that button.

Fusang asked why.

He said, Do you plan to hold on to that thing for the rest of your life? He had continued, I love you, you must know that.

Looking at herself in the mirror several days later, Fusang said, I love you, you must know that. She didn't know why she was smiling, smiling and shaking her head at herself for smiling.

Checking her makeup one last time, she looped a garland of silk flowers reserved for formal occasions around her bun and went downstairs.

Da Yong was just coming in the door. He stepped forward and took her arm. He was wearing a long pale cotton gown; the only flash on him now came from his teeth. When they entered the opera house, the crowd respectfully parted for them. Everyone knew he would announce Fusang's freedom tonight. She was his last remaining prostitute. No longer did anyone shout, Hey Da Yong, you're not dead!

No longer did he banter back, I'd hate to die and leave your son without a daddy!

Da Yong grimaced, embarrassed along with everyone else by how proper he had become.

No one knew what had made him suddenly start performing good deeds. Some said that he had been talking with the foreign church, that someone had seen him sneaking out the back door. Others guessed that his dead mother had met a ghost in the underworld with a grievance against her son, who pestered her to the point that she finally appeared to Da Yong in a dream to get him to mend his ways in this world so she could get some peace and quiet in the next.

Others were saying that he wanted to be ready to meet his wife. She was looking for him and he was looking for her, and they might find each other any day, so he couldn't very well be doing something immoral the very first time she laid eyes on him. It was also said that he was tracking down anyone who knew where his wife was and killing him, because it was common knowledge his wife had been sold to a brothel.

When Da Yong and Fusang reached their box to the left of the stage, an attendant brought tea and dried fruit for them and lit Da Yong's cigar. The attendant was about to let down the curtain when Da Yong said, We won't see a thing, leave it up. The attendant was torn for a moment, then realized Fusang wasn't an ordinary, respectable woman and didn't need to be shielded from men's eyes.

Fusang fanned herself and Da Yong with a silk fan.

Da Yong turned to look at her and she met his eyes. He couldn't resist looking at her again. Really, she was as radiant as a goddess.

He took her hand, his head swimming, suddenly remembering that when the opera let out tonight, she wouldn't have to leave with him. With a wave of sorrow, he reluctantly dropped her hand. Then it occurred to him that Fusang ought to be his wife; she had everything one could ever want in a wife. Thinking further, he realized that wasn't right; Fusang would make a terrible wife, because she was such an outstanding prostitute. She could never be a wife. And his wife could never be like her; wife and whore were as far apart as heaven and earth.

There were some white devils in the audience who had learned to say things like *hello, thank you,* and *I like Chinese girls,* but with a staged bravado or totally unfeigned frivolity. They'd heard that a famous female lead had just arrived from China, whose claim to fame in Guangdong was a waist that slithered like a water snake.

The box across from Da Yong and Fusang remained empty, even when it came time for the opera to start. As the crowd grew more and more restless, the curtain accidentally went up on the famous female lead—female above the waist, male below—catching him right in the midst of gnawing on a roasted goose neck. He froze and he and the audience just looked at each other for a second before the curtain came crashing down.

The whole place erupted with whistling, applause, and the stamping of feet.

Half an hour after the opera was supposed to begin, a bell rang outside the theater. Da Yong thought, Someone even more important than I am has arrived.

Quiet fell as several whites took the box on the right. Everyone recognized the man with the affable face as the owner of the biggest slaughterhouse in the state; he was in the city to hire Chinese. Naturally, the women at his side were his wife and daughter, and the two men behind him were his bodyguards.

They were looking around through their opera glasses before they were even settled in their seats. It wasn't long before the slaughterhouse owner focused upon Fusang's face. Long after the opera began, he still hadn't turned his attention from her face to the stage.

Fusang had no idea that the businessman had such a close view of her through the opera glass. Examining her face, he suddenly realized she was the famous whore responsible for the city's bad reputation. He studied her from head to toe, taking in her famous parts one by one, and then analyzing the reasons for her fame. Her eyes were so beautiful she had to be stupid. The only explanation for the warmth of her smile was that she truly had no shame. And the voluptuousness of her body just proved how wanton she really was. He was still looking at her when he told a bodyguard to go get the house manager.

As the famous female lead took the stage, the musicians sitting immediately behind swung into action and set the volume rising. The clamor in the audience rose along with it. Unable to make out what the businessman was saying, the house manager just kept doffing his cap and bowing.

He heard the last thing he said though, Get them to quiet down!

Everyone, on stage and off, heard it. The place fell still.

The businessman pointed to the box across from him and said, Please ask that woman of ill repute to leave at once. How dare she show herself here for all to see? In front of my wife and daughter!

The manager asked, Where would you like her to go, sir?

I don't care, as long as my wife and daughter don't have to look at her.

The manager returned shortly to the businessman's box and said apologetically, If you don't want to look at her, perhaps you should just keep your eyes on the stage.

Pointing at Fusang, the businessman said, That. . . woman does not belong in public. The minute she walked in this door it was an insult to my wife and daughter. Ask her to leave.

The manager said, She has a ticket just like everyone else.

The wife interjected at this point, For God's sake, we can leave!

The businessman said, No, she must leave at once.

The manager went back to convey the message. The businessman watched through his opera glasses. He saw the big man with the queue pick up his own opera glasses and look over as he listened to the bowing manager.

Through the opera glasses, Da Yong and the businessman were brought nose to nose. Da Yong said to the manager, They can put down their curtain.

The manager conveyed the message.

The businessman shouted across the room to Da Yong, You put down *your* curtain!

The musicians stopped playing when they saw Da Yong jump up. The female lead sang a few lines solo before realizing something was wrong and stopped too. A hush came over the audience.

Da Yong said, We don't mind being seen and we don't mind seeing others. Why should we lower our curtain?

Da Yong's voice wasn't loud, but in the silence of the theater it was deafening.

The businessman asked, Who are you?

Da Yong pulled out his old lewd smile once more. Leaning over the box rail, he said, Need you ask? I'm her lover, Your Excellency.

The wife and daughter gasped.

The businessman stared at this brazen display of shamelessness for a moment and then said, Then I kindly ask the gentleman to see that your lover leaves the premises at once.

Da Yong said, You are mistaken, Your Excellency. She is not mine alone. Ask the bachelors among us if they can bear to see Fusang driven away.

Everyone laughed. The whites in the audience shrieked.

The businessman said, This city is a disgrace! And we have people like you to thank for it!

Da Yong said, You flatter me, Your Excellency.

If you do not remove this fallen woman from my sight at once, said the businessman, I will be forced to take other measures.

On what grounds, Your Excellency?

The businessman smiled coldly, Her status.

What status is that, Your Excellency?

A prostitute! A fallen woman in red!

Once more you are mistaken, Your Excellency. As of now, Miss Fusang is just like your wife and daughter, or rather, a better woman than they.

The daughter gasped, My God!

Da Yong addressed the shaved heads in the theater, Everyone listen. From now on, Fusang sits at the same table as your mother, godmother, sister, or wife! He turned back to the businessman: Your Excellency, may we return to the show now?

No.

Da Yong noticed the two bodyguards taking their pistols from their holsters, loading them, and coming toward Fusang.

The manager said to Da Yong, Back off or we're going to have another riot on our hands; this is the only theater we've got and we've only just replaced the doors from last time.

Ignoring him, Da Yong kept his eyes on the bodyguards crossing the stage. He gave the manager a push and said, Out of my way or I might beat you up too while I'm at it.

The bodyguards beckoned to Fusang with one hand and aimed their pistols at her with the other, We have orders to throw you out.

Fusang looked at Da Yong. A bead of sweat trickled down his hairline. She looked at the bodyguards.

Everyone in the theater was watching her.

She slowly and deliberately rose from her seat. The bodyguards turned to see her out.

Da Yong threw both fists at once, one to each side. A gun was deflected as it went off and the manager got shot in the belly. Da Yong snatched the gun from the floor and bolted down the stairs.

He leapt from bench to bench and ran through the stampeding crowd for the door. The businessman and his family had already left. Da Yong grabbed him when he had one foot in the carriage.

Don't shoot! Don't shoot!

Shooting is too good for you.

He tossed the gun over his head onto the roof.

By the time the carriage turned around and came charging back, it was pretty much all over for the slaughterhouse owner. While the wife and daughter remained in the carriage, Da Yong hurriedly wiped the blood from the businessman's face and brought the bow tie that had twisted to the back of his neck around to the front again. He took off running, but his foot hit one of the businessman's shoes. He picked it up and put it back on the businessman's foot. When he looked up, he was surrounded by police on horseback. Da Yong had never seen the police out in such unified force.

THIS TIME THE POLICE EXERCISED considerable diligence with Da Yong. They excavated their stacks of case files like archaeologists and discovered Da Yong wasn't Da Yong at all, but someone who had disappeared and reappeared many times. A man would have to become many men in order to pull off this many crimes.

This Da Yong had a record: racetrack fraud, slave trafficking, murder.

When he heard these verdicts, his heart sank, Was that all?

On the afternoon his sentence of hanging was announced, Fusang brought him two good cigars when she visited.

His hair was a mess and his queue was crooked. Fusang took his ox horn comb from her bag.

He smiled and turned around so she could pull his hair through the bars to comb it. When he noticed the trouble she was having, he got down on one knee. Before long, he was kneeling on both knees, sitting on his heels.

Eyeing the guard two paces away, Fusang pulled out her silk handkerchief and stuffed it into Da Yong's hand. She knew he would wet it with spittle and wipe the blood from his face. She knew he didn't like anyone to have gaping wounds or messy hair and a dirty face. Now his own wounds gaped and his hair was a mess and his face was dirty.

Kneeling with his back to her, Da Yong spoke half-heartedly of his regrets. He should have killed her so he wouldn't have to keep worrying about her from the other side.

Fusang silently and gratefully brought the comb through the bars again and again, giving extra attention to the itchy spots on his scalp, carefully skirting the in-juries.

He turned back with a start to find himself kneeling and Fusang standing.

I CANNOT BELIEVE my eyes. You don't look the least bit distressed. Such an enormous turn of events. Why are you so calm?

More and more I find that I don't understand you. That there's no way to understand you. Reading between the lines of all those histories, I figured out your ignorance and simplicity from the beginning, but later I had to wonder whether the reason you never hid your interest in sex was some mild form of retardation that just kept you from knowing any better. Then I decided that you were more serious than most women about commitment and that you kept your true feelings hidden because they were for Chris and Chris alone. But what you've decided to do about Chris and Da Yong now just confuses me all over again. Your smile makes me suspect that I have never known a thing about you.

I can't believe that one hundred and sixty books don't offer enough information to understand someone like you.

I can't believe that over a century later, you are nothing more than what those writers understood of you then: "This beautiful prostitute mysteriously appeared in this port, so many things mysteriously revolved around her, and then she mysteriously disappeared."

You should know that I can't stand a mystery. Even if I write you off as one, I still have to have some basic grasp of what's behind it. But your smile and the look in your eyes now don't even give me that. You see how upset I am, yet you just go on fanning yourself with that silk fan of yours. This is the way you've always looked at people in distress or in a fistfight, for that matter: smiling as if you weren't quite there, with just a trace of surprise and a trace of pity. You make it seem like *they* are the mystery.

I suspect that you figured out a long time ago who Da

Yong was. When he gave you this silver bracelet, you knew where its mate was. These are crude handmade pieces, one with a dragon's head, the other a tiger's, but only recognizable as such by the old country silversmith who made them. You started wearing yours when you were two, the one with the tiger. When you outgrew it and even the silversmith couldn't enlarge it anymore, you kept it with you. You never lost it all this time, as if it just refused to be lost.

The one Da Yong gave you now was bigger, the one with the dragon. When he handed it to you, his eyes studied your face, but his tone was unexpectedly flippant: Go cash it in for a bowl of fish congee. It was his last piece of jewelry.

You knew he was sounding you out.

He'd often asked about your background. You never told him much.

So the relationship between you and Da Yong is clear now. But what about you and Chris?

When you reach the school, you hear the tattoo of marching drums coming from the yard. You look through the gate and see all the girls standing in a circle around Chris. There are thirty-some girls, the youngest not more than eleven or twelve, each with an old marching drum at her waist. When Chris shouts a command, the girls beat the drums and laugh, laugh till they roll all over the ground with laughter.

Chris keeps a stern face at first, but can't hold it long

before he too is laughing like a fool, laughing and chasing the girls who used their drumsticks on his head.

You laugh too. For a long time.

When Chris is lifted off the ground by several girls, he is laughing and scolding, his face bright red, but before long he breaks free and goes on the attack. Everyone is covered with dirt, their faces sweaty.

When it is about to get dark, Chris picks up his jacket and says something to the girls. One of them tells him he has dirt on his back and he turns around to let her brush it off.

Now they are coming toward you. You quickly turn away, because you see once again that gaze of Chris's that looks but doesn't seem to see. As you turn your face to the wall, the man lighting the gaslights raises a long pole above your head. You know Chris is going to walk right by you again.

Their chirping and chattering draws nearer. In the sound of all those footsteps you make out Chris's. He's walked with the same long loose stride ever since he was a boy. He is actually much more arrogant than anyone, including himself, realizes. You and I see it, though, for where else would this knowing smile of ours be coming from?

You hear his steps shorten as he draws closer, shorten and seem to delay. Then there is a brief pause or perhaps it is not a pause at all, merely an errant beat in your hearts. And then, just as I predicted, he walks right past you.

You feel a pang. Or maybe you don't—I'm not sure I can guess what is going through your mind right now. I'm not even sure what prompted you to go to the school. I don't know whether you intended to start something with him or end it. It seemed like you came to tell him about your relationship with Da Yong and what you were going to do about it, but then he saved you the trouble.

Looking at your feet, you wish for the first time they were big, to follow those girls.

Or maybe you don't think that at all. I've got this bad habit of having to orchestrate and analyze everyone's thinking all the time. You aren't thinking anything; your mind is completely blank.

Chris suddenly turns around, one hundred and eighty degrees, toward you.

You hear him panting and then calling to you. While you are still deciding whether to turn your head, he is standing in front of you. There is no distance at all between you now. When his breath touches your temples, the last thing you see is his chest pushing toward you from the inside, pushing closer to you. You turn your head.

In that same moment he takes your hand. You look at your hand in his tight grasp.

The girls have noticed that something is happening and stop, craning their bodies, their necks, their faces. They all seem to be looking askance at you.

Chris drops your hand and then clasps it again more emphatically.

The gray cotton uniforms of the students stiffen as if frozen. They have forgotten that they should never show such brazen shock or disgust. They have forgotten that what they are really staring at is themselves, that so many of them just two or three years ago had called out, Chinese girl nice, hey mister, come and see.

But you don't even notice them. You just feel Chris's hand growing colder and starting to tremble.

Holding your hand with resolve, he is pulling you toward them. His resolve is meant to challenge them. And to sacrifice himself. His martyred resolve is turning his hand as cold as the mud at the bottom of an icy river. His resolve forces the girls to abandon their judgmental stares and dissolve into poses of gradual acceptance of you.

Chris, however, does not take you into their midst. He slows down and turns to look at you, his face white as paper in the twilight. He has become a handsome, arrogant man; we both have to admit that.

Men just off work are coming out of the cigar and shoe factories, exhausted, trailing their bedraggled queues. When they see you and Chris holding hands, their eyes double in size. The shock alone boosts their sagging spirits.

Chris pulls you closer to him, nearly embraces you. He hates the fact that the workers are shocked and his pale young face glows with righteousness. He is totally unaware of what he has been saying over and over again, from the moment he took your hand: Fusang, we'll make a life together. I want everyone to know. I'll take you to Montana, where whites and colored people can get married.

The expression on his face and these repeated declarations of his bring to mind the self-importance of people who devote their lives to a cause. The wind is blowing his thick blond hair back, exposing his broad forehead. His face reminds me of idealists through the ages, whatever their cause: the claim that the earth revolves around the sun, the theory of evolution, the Paris Commune, the October Revolution, the Three People's Principles, communism.. . .It is as if his being with you, Fusang, is not a matter of anything so shallow as love or happiness, but rather a grand sacrifice. Or perhaps when love reaches this stage it crowds out ordinary feelings and becomes a doctrine, an ideal, that can only be realized through sacrifice. He is using you to enact his sacrifice for the ideal of love. He also wants to show everyone of his race and yours that his self-sacrifice will form a bridge across the racial divide. Through you he can sacrifice himself and redeem his race for its crimes against you; he would give a lifetime, no, make that three, to atone for the gang rape during the riot. Your love is no longer a private matter between the two of you, for he has announced it to the world, to all these narrow-minded, prejudiced faces, white and yellow alike.

Chris is holding your hand and walking with you, through the incomprehension and disgust of the students, through the shock of the cigar factory workers—if they saw a dog mating a cat they could not have been more shocked. Chris is walking as if marching in protest, having forgotten that the reason he came back for you was love and love alone.

Or maybe I'm wrong again and Chris wasn't thinking about sacrifice and redemption at all. My interpretations of white people are usually based on Chinese thinking. Maybe Chris wasn't thinking so hard. Maybe all he was thinking about was having a good time with you tonight, with Da Yong out of the way. Da Yong will be hanged tomorrow morning at ten—it's been in all the papers.

And it was a good night. Neither of you spoke much. The two of you have found that with the language difference not speaking at all is the best communication. There are no misunderstandings with silence. It is perfectly exact.

You went to a little restaurant. The waiter knew you and brought out a plate of river snails before you even ordered. They were still warm and had probably been alive right up to the moment they hit the plate. Chris's mischievous streak came out again as he tried to pick up the slippery shells with chopsticks, never managing once to get one all the way to his mouth. When one chopstick crept out past the other, he pushed it back in line with the index finger of his left hand. You picked up a snail with your chopsticks, sucked off the juice, poked the tip of your chopstick through the opening that had been cut near the tail, and sucked out the head. Chris's jaw gaped as he watched, fascinated by the agility of your lips and tongue. He reached under the table and found your knee.

It was a good night, so good it seemed to portend something. He had fallen asleep in your arms. In the morning you had a problem—all those kisses and you still couldn't get him to let you go. He slept so soundly, like all young men. You finally pulled yourself free and were about to stand up when you leaned back down and pulled your hair bit by bit from his grasp. His grip was so tight that you couldn't pull the last lock free. You turned and found the scissors on the dressing table. You cut the hair, leaving that last lock in his hand forever.

Yes, I said forever. I can already see where this is going. The carriage is taking you to the gallows. It's a long way; you can take your time fixing your hair, powdering your face, making yourself up in style. The matron you hired corrects you without saying a word—she was a bride once. The canopy is on the seat beside you.

You put on the gown of thick satin, embroidered with ten catties of colorful floss. You look glorious. You keep wanting to run your fingers over your dress, the way I have the derelict urge to touch things in a museum.

When the driver brings the carriage to a stop, you hear the ocean wind roar.

DA YONG WAS WEARING fifty pounds of manacles and leg irons, and a black satin mandarin jacket over a long gown of gray wool. His hair was neatly combed even if it was filthy and the fragrant oil in his queue made it hang straight and heavy all the way past his waist. Several guards had been handpicked to escort Da Yong to the gallows and now they surrounded him, their steps cautious as they took him from his cell.

He pulled a cigar butt from behind his ear and asked for a light.

The guards admired Da Yong. Because his life had been a grand show and his death would be too. Also because when he was surrounded by the police, he had neither surrendered nor resisted, but simply obeyed the law with dignity. And because it was only after his arrest that the police discovered the daggers at his waist—he could have used them all along to try to get away.

One of the guards pulled out his matches, lit one, and then lit Da Yong's cigar, his whole body cautious and defensive.

Da Yong laughed and said, This long drawn-out dying sure gets on your nerves, doesn't it?

The guard said, Yes, sirree.

Da Yong said, A wedding would really liven things up around here, don't you think?

The guard said, Yes, indeed.

The wind was roaring. It bore in the sound of horns, then changed direction and sent the music somewhere else.

Da Yong saw Fusang approaching with her escort.

Walking toward him on a length of red satin, she was all decked out, her head covered with the red phoenix facing the rising sun veil. The canopy was set up across from the gallows.

The grounds were roped off and a crowd was gathered behind the ropes. Most of the crowd was Chinese, but there were also several white reporters. Everyone's clothes were flapping in the wind. But coins were sewn all over Fusang's veil and the wind couldn't budge it.

With Da Yong in front and Fusang a few feet behind him, each of them holding a ribbon from the big satin flower suspended between them, they walked to the canopy and knelt before it. Da Yong turned out to be a most proper bridegroom—his eyes never left Fusang, even when his leg irons almost tripped him.

A guard came over and adjusted the leg irons so Da Yong could kneel more comfortably.

When the veil was pulled off, the crowd gasped. Fusang was so beautiful some people started to cry.

Da Yong smiled as he looked at his bride. He could thoroughly imagine her pushing the millstone, chopping firewood, shouldering baskets on a carrying pole. The Fusang he saw was beating laundry at the river, shelling peas on the threshold, waiting for him to come home. He could see the women lined up on the riverbank and Fusang running out from their midst to meet not the postman, but him, Da Yong, home at last. This was Da Yong at sixty and meeting him was Fusang at fifty.

Seeing all these things, he said to her, Take your time, live a good, long life. I can wait for you.

Fusang said, I'll take you home.

Scatter half in the ocean.

Okay. What about the other half?

Da Yong hesitated. Scatter it on my mother's grave. He laughed. She'll recognize me.

SQUEEZING THROUGH THE CROWD, Chris saw the ship move.

He pushed his way to the front, bumping backs and shoulders and stepping on feet as he ran down the uneven stone steps of the dock.

He watched Fusang, dressed in red, standing on deck, growing smaller. He saw the urn of Da Yong's ashes in her arms, covered in red silk, topped with a Chinese bridegroom's cap.

Chris learned from the newspaper what Fusang did after she left him that morning. She had left that lock of black hair in his hand and cut herself free from him just like that.

The paper had printed a photograph of the gallows wedding and reported that the bride would be sailing on June thirtieth to take her husband's ashes home.

Chris realized that he had never, ever understood Fusang.

Roughly six months later, he happened to pass Fusang's house and found it no longer deserted as it had been for quite some time. Once more there was a long line of men at the door.

He stood there stunned for a long time and then walked to the end of the line. All the men looked at him. He held his ground and looked right back at them.

When his turn came, the doorman (one Chris had never seen before) said to him politely, I'm sorry, sir, we don't take whites.

Sure enough, there wasn't a single white in the line. No wonder they were looking at him that way.

He said, I'm a friend of hers. She asked me to come.

He dodged the doorman and ran up the stairs. The door was half-shut and he slammed it open.

A woman jerked around to face him. She wasn't Fusang. She was fifteen or sixteen, a slip of a girl.

But he had already blurted out Fusang's name.

The doorman had followed him up and said to him gently, Fusang's gone; she's been gone a long time now.

CHRIS THOUGHT OF FUSANG again the day before he died. He was seventy-five. He still had that lock of her hair. He realized that when she cut the two of them apart, she was also cutting all ties.

Marrying Da Yong right before his death was a way to protect herself forever. She had never loved Da Yong, alive or dead.

Chris also thought about his life, the life that Fusang had changed. He'd spent it fighting the persecution of the Chinese and the violence among the Chinese. He had become a Chinese history professor. He felt Fusang watching everything he did. Whether she approved or not, she was always watching him.

His fifty years of a happy marriage and family life bore out Fusang's wisdom: Marriage had protected him forever from love.

I TOLD MY WHITE HUSBAND that I was writing about him. He said, Great! At least this is something we can share. It will become part of our history together.

He was the one who dug through every library in San Francisco to bring me all these books with mentions of you.

Listen to this description of you in your old age: "At nearly ninety, she dresses in a plain-colored cheongsam with a subtle pattern, the fabric of the highest quality; her silver hair is coiled into an enormous chignon—most of it obviously not her own.. . .No one knows how this woman who once starred in so many farces (or shall we say tragedies?) spent the rest of her life, but clearly, of the three thousand Chinese prostitutes who came to these shores, she is one of the ones who lived the longest."

Other books have this to say about you: "A little eatery cropped up near the banking district; its proprietress looked to be in her sixties. She was rumored to be the Fusang who was once so famous. Customers line up all the way out the door, but she has never expanded the place."

And then there are sources that portray you in ways

new to me: "In her seventies, she sits at a fruit stand peeling pineapples. She is shabbily dressed and seems pre-occupied when she waits on the occasional customer."

All these different renditions of your old age make you smile. It turns out that there can be so many different versions of the same historical event.

That's why my history and my husband's will never be the same.

Regardless of all these different descriptions, all I can be sure of is the you right in front of me. Come a little closer, toward the lamp. Excellent. Now I can smell the fragrance of your hair.

That reminds me, do you still have that brass button of Chris's in your bun? Just how long do you plan to keep it? Will you keep it right along with all these different versions of your history?

The way Chris is keeping that lock of your hair.

One day you were hurrying down the steps of the Church of the Blessed Virgin and a tall thin old man passed you on his way up. His white hair was blown out of place by the wind. That was Chris. You didn't recognize each other.

Another time, you saw an old couple and a young man getting out of a parked car. The young man looked familiar to you. You waited until they were gone before you remembered that he reminded you of Chris. He was called Chris too, carrying on his father's name.

At random, yet by destiny, you and Chris would come

from your different worlds to the same place, run into each other and miss each other, neither of you giving the other a second glance.

Sometimes my heart leaps into my throat because you nearly look back and he almost stops. But it always turns out that you miss each other.

This time I'm determined you won't. Chris's wife has just passed away; the woman with him is his daughter. He wants to go to Chinatown for lunch. You are sitting at a table in a corner of the crowded restaurant, already finished with your meal, picking at the last of the river snails for something to do. He and his daughter come up to ask whether this is the only restaurant that sells snails. You smile and nod. He asks if they can share your table. You say, Of course. He sees you sucking a snail shell and turns with a smile to his daughter and whispers in her ear. Something doesn't feel right to you and you call for your check. He suddenly looks at you. Maybe the sound of your voice has reminded him. When his food comes, you watch him too, hoping that one of his chopsticks will creep past the other and he will stop and push it back with the index finger of his left hand. But he is quite good with chopsticks, nearly as good as you. Of course after all this time he would be. You slowly pick up the last snail, poke the tail with a chopstick, and bring it to your mouth. He happens to look up and your eyes meet.

I have to wonder whether your failure to recognize each other was intentional. You took your check, paid, and walked toward the door. When you reached it you looked back, but all he gave you was the back of his head. Yet as soon as you turned around again, he turned to look at you. All he saw was your back as you hobbled away.

A selected list of titles available from
Faber and Faber Ltd

Paul Auster	*The New York Trilogy*	0–571–15223–6
Peter Carey	*Jack Maggs*	0–571–19377–3
Peter Carey	*Oscar and Lucinda*	0–571–15304–6
Peter Carey	*True History of the Kelly Gang*	0–571–20987–4
Mavis Cheek	*Mrs Fytton's Country Life*	0–571–20541–0
Joseph Connolly	*Summer Things*	0–571–19574–1
Michael Dibdin	*Dead Lagoon*	0–571–17347–0
Giles Foden	*The Last King of Scotland*	0–571–19564–4
Michael Frayn	*Headlong*	0–571–20147–4
William Golding	*Lord of the Flies*	0–571–19147–9
Andrew Greig	*That Summer*	0–571–20473–2
Kazuo Ishiguro	*The Remains of the Day*	0–571–15491–3
Kazuo Ishiguro	*When We Were Orphans*	0–571–20516–x
P. D. James	*An Unsuitable Job for a Woman*	0–571–20389–2
Barbara Kingsolver	*The Poisonwood Bible*	0–571–20175–x
Barbara Kingsolver	*Prodigal Summer*	0–571–20648–4
Milan Kundera	*Immortality*	0–571–14456–x
Milan Kundera	*The Unbearable Lightness of Being*	0–571–13539–0
Hanif Kureishi	*The Buddha of Suburbia*	0–571–14274–5
Hanif Kureishi	*Intimacy*	0–571–19570–9
John Lanchester	*Mr Phillips*	0–571–20171–7
John McGahern	*Amongst Women*	0–571–16160–x
Rohinton Mistry	*A Fine Balance*	0–571–17936–3
Lorrie Moore	*Birds of America*	0–571–19727–2
Andrew O'Hagan	*Our Fathers*	0–571–20106–7
Sylvia Plath	*The Bell Jar*	0–571–08178–9
Jane Smiley	*Horse Heaven*	0–571–20560–7
Banana Yoshimoto	*Kitchen*	0–571–17104–4

In case of difficulty in purchasing any Faber title through normal channels, books can be purchased from:

Bookpost, PO BOX 29, Douglas, Isle of Man, IM99 1BQ

Credit cards accepted. Please telephone 01624 836000, fax 01624 837033
Internet www.bookpost.co.uk *or* email bookshop@enterprise.net for details.